the WHITEMOON CRISIS

by
FRANK MOSCO

USA

Quillquest Books

A division of Quillquest Enterprises.
Quillquest Books, Quillquest Junior Books and the sailing quill are the exclusive
trademarks of Quillquest Enterprises.

This book is a work of fiction.
Names, characters, businesses, organizations, places, events, and
incidents are either the product of the author's imagination or are used
fictitiously. Any resemblance to actual persons, living or dead, events, or
locales is entirely coincidental.

ISBN 0-9769272-0-9 Quillquest Books, 2004
Second edition, paperback

ISBN 0-9769272-3-3 Quillquest Books, 2006
Second edition, hardback

ISBN 0-940075-00-8 Skipjack Books, 1986
First edition, paperback

Dedicated to:

Charlotte Smith of GCS, who lit the flame
&
Kathy Mills-Hayes of JC, who fueled the fire.

the WHITEMOON CRISIS

Prologue

The classic yacht cut steadily through the sea utilizing only a small portion of the actual power of her engines. She was ghostly with running lights and all other lights off save for one small red lamp in the bridge; which reflected along the shiny mahogany trim like slow neon. The sea was reasonably calm as far as the eye permitted and the gray clouds that came with nightfall hid the moon. Were it not for the white water of the break at her bow as she split the surface the yacht would be completely undetectable. Her Captain glared into the darkness, his mind and senses giving way to fantasy. He felt as though he were in some mystic craft floating through space, alone, free, independent of all he despised in life and wondering if death offered such tranquility.

"Want me to relieve you, sir?"

The young voice was subtle, however it pierced the Captain's state of mind and sent a pain of reality to the back of his neck. He raised a hand from the wheel and massaged it slowly. The pain persisted.

"Sir, would you like me to take the wheel for awhile?" the crewman repeated.

"No. It's almost time for the drop. How 'bout some coffee" he suggested.

"Sure thing," the young crewman said as he started from the bridge. "Be back in a minute."

Catching a glimpse of a sweeping light in the distance to the northwest the Captain reached for a cigarette, lit it, then picked up a phone connecting him with below.

"Yes sir?" came a voice from the other end.

"Twenty minutes. Make ready," he ordered, then replaced the phone, focused on the beacon of the distant lighthouse and tried his best to return to his fantasy. It was a failed effort.

Below, two men huddled over a large torpedo-like object, setting dials inside its open panel. They concentrated intensely to insure that all systems and settings were precise.

"That's it," said one as he sat back in relief.

The other closed and secured the panel. "Damn genius, those Navy boys," he commented as they slid the object into the launch tube.

On the bridge a red light blinked on the Captain's phone. "Yes," he answered.

"It's all yours, Captain."

"Stand by," the Captain ordered then replaced the receiver, put out his cigarette and began changing course. They were heading due north. Having the lighthouse directly west of them, he brought the craft about and headed straight for the coast. After a few minutes and judging the distance to be about two miles off shore, he cut the engines. Unlocking and opening a compartment resembling the glove compartment of an automobile revealed a dimly lit series of toggle switches and one red button labeled LAUNCH. Showing little enthusiasm, he expertly flipped one switch, then another.

Below the waterline of the yacht a circular portion of the hull slid aside exposing a bow tube much like that of a submarine. A green light on the panel blinked indicating to the Captain all was ready. He glanced over his shoulder to a tall shadowed man quietly poised on the port side of the bridge. The man turned and braced himself on a rail then nodded approval.

The Captain pushed the launch button and the yacht shuddered slightly as the cylindrical object propelled itself into the black night sea. It shot out of the hull of the yacht with exceptional speed, even more exceptional was its lack of noise. Running just below the surface it jetted swiftly and precisely toward the barrier island beach and the lighthouse.

Below, the two technicians hovered over an instrument panel, tracking, timing and measuring distance.

"Cut it," ordered one as they watched the instruments intently for the cylinders reaction.

The hissing jet propulsion ceased and the cylinder nosed down. Upon impact with the sandy bottom the nose exploded, sending a small anchor into the ocean floor.

"It's secure," stated one of the men.

"Activate it," ordered the other.

"Secure and activated," came the reply as the task was completed.

The phone on the bridge lit once again.

"It's all set, sir."

The Captain turned to the shadowed figure behind him, motioned with a nod that all was well then replaced the phone. For a moment he fixed his attention on the man's face as the lighthouse beacon swept across the sky and for that moment he felt possessed as if he were being cursed. Nothing, he thought, nothing ever changes that man's eyes. He's a goddamn devil.

The moon slid from behind a cloud as the yacht came about and headed out to sea.

"Son of a bitch," the Captain mouthed quietly to himself, remembering his employer's eyes. The man is insane.

The engines surged as the propellers of the one hundred twenty foot craft gripped the dark salty water and pushed them into the night. Behind them on the ocean floor, a few hundred feet from the secluded sandy beach of St. Augustine, Florida, the cylinder lay secure and anchored against the tide. A steady deep-throated sound came from within… like that of a tiger on the prowl.

Chapter One

It was early morning and the inlet waters across the street had just come alive with the tide. There were few clouds in the sky indicating it would be a good day but the Florida heat was already becoming dominant. The boy sat Indian style on the lawn in front of his home and gazed impatiently down the street while eating a peanut butter and banana sandwich. Washing it down with a swig of Coke he hoped his father wouldn't notice what he had fixed himself for breakfast. When his gaze returned from the street he focused on the sleek new surfboard laying next to him glistening in the morning sun, its skeg extended upward like the dorsal fin of a shark. He checked his shirt pocket, assuring himself for the third time he hadn't forgotten his board wax. He'd been sitting there for nearly a half hour now, listening to the sounds of cartoons drift from the den of the house and watching the pelicans crash dive into the inlet for their morning meal.

The smell of coffee made its way from the kitchen. Dad is up now, he thought as he visualized his father stumbling from the bedroom to the den. He would turn down the television and habitually ask his little brother if he had brushed his teeth. His father would then drudgingly continue to the kitchen, take a swig of orange juice and brew a fresh pot of coffee. The boy lay back on the grass, rested on one elbow and smiled. How many times he'd seen this morning ritual since his mother died. He remembered when the family used to wake up to the aroma of a good hot breakfast. Sausage, waffles, sometimes those French things he couldn't pronounce, but now...

"Chris!" his father's distant voice bellowed through the kitchen window. A faint reply came from his younger brother in the den, intermingled with a cereal commercial.

"Get in here and clean up your mess!"

"Tony did it," replied young Chris accusingly.

Tony cringed as he sat up on the grass. That little fart, he thought angrily, half that mess is his. He contemplated future revenge as he glared back down the street settling his view on the old lighthouse further down the inlet. A few blocks away the front of a rusty old topless 1945 war surplus jeep shot out from behind a growth of weeds and palmettos. Its oversized tires wrrrrd as it barely slowed to make the corner. Tony was on his feet, snatching up the board and jogging to the curb as the jeep rattled to a halt in front of the house.

"Let's go, short stuff, before we lose the tide," shouted the jeep's driver as he struck the horn button. From under the hood an AHOOGA sounded harshly, cutting through the tranquil waterfront neighborhood. He removed his wire-rimmed sunglasses and wiped them clear with his faded blue t-shirt, stretched the shirt to his face and wiped the sweat from around his eyes and forehead. "Nice board," said Blacky, replacing his glasses.

Tony lifted the board carefully to the driver who secured it next to his own against the roll bar then grabbed a canvas bag from the passenger seat and tossed it to the rear of the vehicle. The boy eyed his new board resting next to Blacky's and grinned proudly.

"Nice," Blacky repeated. "Not a ding on it. Not yet anyway." He laughed, slapped the seat and told the boy to hop in.

Just as the boy settled in, the front door of the house opened and a sharp whistle grabbed their attention. His father strolled out and across the lawn to the side of the jeep where he extended with a nod and a cup of coffee a silent good morning.

"You eat any breakfast?" he questioned his son.

"Yeah, dad."

His father squinted into the morning sun, running his fingers through his dirty blond hair, "Listen Blacky, he's a good swimmer but he's still just a kid."

"I'll watch him, Mr. Majors," Blacky assured him. "No sweat."

"Thanks. Appreciate it." Majors looked down to his son, leaned on the roll bar of the jeep and smiled, "You still have to cut the grass when you get back."

"The mower's broke, dad," grinned the boy.

His father offered up a look of defeat to Blacky and shrugged then leaned to his son, said, "Happy birthday," and started to kiss him on the forehead.

"Dad!" the boy said, leaning away in protest.

Understanding his son's embarrassment, Majors settled for a slap on the head. "Be careful," he ordered. "And stay away from those wild women on the beach."

"Dad!"

"Dad!" mimicked Blacky as he revved the engine and threw the jeep into gear. "Listen kid," he said, leaning to Tony in confidence, "I know some really nice ladies down by...

"Later Blacky, later," interrupted the boy's father.

They laughed as the vehicle lurched forward making a 180-degree turn. Blacky hit the ahooga horn again as they rounded the far corner a few blocks away.

Majors stood and watched until his view of the jeep was lost, then gave the inlet and surrounding area a panoramic inspection. He smiled with the satisfaction of his son fully appreciating the birthday present of a new surfboard, knowing it was a gift of culture as much as a big toy.

Fifteen minutes later the jeep turned off the coast road A1A and onto the sandy beach access.

"Why do they call this Conch Island?" asked the boy.

"Used to be an island," answered Blacky. The island expanded and the inlet filled in years ago so now it's part of the rest of Anastasia Island."

"Why don't they dig it out again?"

"Don't know. Cost too much I guess. Beaches change all the time. It's natural. They really screw it up when they start building walls and jetties and stuff. Down by the pier the beach washed away along with some houses during the old hurricane. Hell, they lost most of the pier because of hurricane David and the damn road washed out last year. You just can't hold back old lady nature, man. She's one heavy duty mama. And when it comes to the ocean you either go with the flow or get the hell outa' the way."

"Yeah, hurricane David was funny."

"Funny!" You gotta' be kiddin'."

"Yeah. Dad freaked out and taped all the windows on the house and then when the hurricane was over he couldn't get the tape gunk off. Boy was he pissed. Said he wished they all broke so the insurance could put new ones in."

"Hah, insurance my ass. Insurance money maybe but he probably woulda' got me to do the work."

"Why are we surfing here?" asked Tony as they bumped past the high dunes.

"Well, the waves aren't too big. Good form though and good for little turds like you."

"Crap!" Tony disagreed. "That's pure crap."

"Besides, none of your buddies, who I might add, having been born here and are a little more advanced at the craft than you, will see you eat pie," Blacky laughed.

"What?"

"Eat pie. You know, *bust your ass*."

The boy wondered just how painful and embarrassing eating pie really would be.

Blacky's jeep skidded to a halt near a large dune. He cut the engine and hopped out.

"Is this it?" the boy asked.

"Well it ain't Disney World," Blacky proclaimed as he removed his board from the jeep. "Listen, man, don't sweat it. This is day-one. You've got a million more to go. When you get better I'll take you down to Sebastian Inlet or maybe even up to Hatteras."

"Dad said you surfed up at Ponte Vedra during the hurricane."

"Sure did. Me and a couple other guys. Big ass swells, dude."

"He said... um."

Blacky finished waxing his board, picked it up and tucked it under his arm. "He said what?"

"I don't think I should repeat it."

"Hey, come on kid. Haven't you ever heard of the First Amendment? Said what?"

"Well, he said you were a bunch of crazy, um..."

"Never mind. I think I got the drift. Wax it up and come on out," Blacky laughed as he strutted toward the surf. "You'll be as crazy as the rest of us pretty soon. Then he'll really have something to bitch about."

Just off the beach the waves were well formed but not very challenging. Nothing to get excited and write home about thought Blacky, but just right for the kid. Blacky knew the boy well enough not to concern himself greatly about the basics. He was strong and gutsy for a ten year old. He would pick up surfing quickly and by the end of the summer probably be an uppity little rat-ass surfer like the rest of them.

Tony watched as Blacky entered the water and checked out his style. He did everything well with the ease and grace of a true athlete and the boy was extremely fond of him. He was a friend of his father, a distant cousin, who just showed up at his mother's funeral and has been a regular family feature ever since. It was a big brother relationship made even better by Blacky's informality. Much better, thought the boy, than the more formal attentions of his mother's relatives from up Boston way. They always seemed to be trying to impress each other, even when they talked to the kids in the family. It was decent, he thought, maybe it was even proper but it was boring. That's why I married your dad, his mother told him, because he could match wits with the best of Boston and still not care about spilling spaghetti sauce of his sweatshirt. Tony wasn't exactly sure what she meant by that but he was sure he liked the way she smiled when she said it.

The seasoned surfer pushed his board ahead of him as he entered the water. When he was waist deep he easily slid on to it and began to paddle, stroking long, sliding through the oncoming breakers, white curls of water dousing him and the board.

Tony finished waxing his board and tried to tuck it under his arm but found it was too wide. Instead he hauled it up over his head and started for the surf. Blacky was now sitting up just beyond the swells, waiting for the boy's arrival. He raised his arms like a triumphant boxer then cupped his hands at the corners of his mouth, shouting, "Lets go kid! I'm gettin' old waitin' out here."

Suddenly Blacky's expression changed to surprise. His hands shot to the board in an effort to balance himself and he desperately searched the water around him. He was confused as the board seemed to be moving backwards and before he could belly down and paddle away it began to jerk violently. He held tight, was abruptly overturned and literally yanked under the water, instantly becoming disoriented as he tumbled out of control. Fighting furiously to find the surface, large metal crab-like arms encircled, trapped and crushed him, inflicting extreme pain as it snapped his hip and ribs. The pain caused him to impulsively open his mouth to scream. His lungs filled with water. Desperation and panic crawled over him until his senses gave way to rambling memories. Then the memories faded completely as his world became a dark, silent death.

Tony stood in knee-deep water, his board still above his head. He stared at the surf, searching, questioning what he had just witnessed but through the sound of crashing waves the realization of what happened came to him. He dropped the board and screamed for Blacky. Searching the surf, he began sporadically making his way through the water, all the while getting in deeper without realizing what he was doing, then suddenly, dark tanned wrinkled arms reached out and grabbed him around the waist.

Chapter Two

Majors had come out of the shower and settled down in the den with his second cup of coffee and his youngest son Chris when the phone rang.

"You get it," he told the boy jokingly. "It's probably your girlfriend anyway."

Chris jumped to his feet from in front of the television, "Which one?" he questioned seriously.

This caught Majors off guard. Damn, he thought, the kid's only seven years old. He tried to remember when he first became aware of the opposite sex many years ago but his thoughts were interrupted.

"It's for you."

"Who is it?"

"A man."

"Oh, you're a lot of help," said Majors as he took the phone.

"Well, it's not my girlfriend," the boy replied indifferently as he returned to the Godzilla cartoon on the television.

"Hello," Majors greeted as he thoughtlessly observed Godzilla eliminate three giant alien robots.

"Frank. Roger here. Listen buddy, I need a favor."

Roger was the editor of the local newspaper. He and Frank Majors had become fairly good friends since Majors and his boys moved down from New York two years earlier.

"Good morning Rog," replied Majors, ignoring the request.

"Frank, there's something going on at the beach and I don't have anybody to cover it."

"How the hell are you this bright sunny morning, Rog?" asked Majors, hinting that before making a request it would be nice to at least extend a few howdy-does first.

"Frank, I need…"

"Rog, I have better things to do on Saturday than cover Frisbee tournaments and sand castle contests."

"Come on Frank, I'm serious. It's a drowning or something. I just got a call from Steve."

"Sounds messy. I don't do messy any more. Can't you cover it yourself?"

"Of course not. I'm an editor. Editors don't do that kind of thing."

"You're forgetting your roots, ole buddy. Losing touch with your journalistic past."

"I'll make room for your story," stated Roger, ignoring Majors comments.

"My story?"

"Frank, I've no one available. Besides, it's an easy twenty bucks. How 'bout it?'

"Rog, I haven't even had breakfast, I've got to fix my lawn mower, Chris and I are in the middle of a Saturday morning TV monster massacre and twenty bucks is damn insulting." He knew he would accept the assignment if only as a favor to his poker buddy but he wasn't going to make it easy for the simple reason than to discourage similar future request.

Roger knew the dance and went along. He knew Majors missed his career as a network reporter and could never refuse a chance to show off his reporting expertise, even for a small town rag. He also knew Majors would come through with a good piece.

"Frank, it's probably the only decent story I'll have all week. Who knows, maybe Jaws has come south for a vacation."

"He wouldn't dare," said Majors. "The rates are too high."

"Don't knock it," Roger replied. "This town survives on Yankee pilgrims."

"A bottle of scotch and you're on," Majors bargained.

"Okay damnit. But will you hustle. I'd like to beat the Times on this one."

"The Times own you people, Rog."

"They may own the paper but that doesn't mean I have to kiss their ass."

Majors smiled into the phone. He knew Roger hated the Times attitude toward their "little sister down there". It didn't take much to set him off when it came to management politics.

"I've heard it all before, Rog. Now, you want to fill me in on this story. Little unimportant things like what country, what state, what beach."

"Steve will fill you in. He's on his way to pick you up."

"You bastard!" exclaimed Majors, looking to see if Chris had caught his profanity only to find the boy was mesmerized by some sort of bubbly brew commercial for kids only. He then heard a brief burst of a siren in front of his house. It was Steve. "You bastard, you knew I would go."

"Don't complain buddy. You've got a bottle of scotch coming, remember."

"Yeah, right. And who will drink most of it at the next poker game?" He hung up the telephone and turned to Chris. "I'm going to the beach with Steve for a while."

The boy didn't reply. Godzilla was at it again.

"When your brother gets home, tell him to see if he can get that mower going."

Still getting no response from his son, Majors lifted his arms high above his head and let out a monstrous sound closely resembling the cartoon Godzilla and proceeded to attack. The boy screamed as he was snatched up by an arm and leg and thrown onto the sofa.

"Stand clear kid and I'll blast that big ugly sucker with my laser gun!"

Both Majors and the boy paused and turned in unison to the doorway to find Steve ready in the firing position, wide-eyed and finger extended. They both cracked up, "You look ridiculous," laughed Majors.

"Just doin' my duty here, Mr. Godzilla," returned the St. Johns County deputy. "Speakin' of duty, you 'bout ready to ride there, Clark Kent?"

"Yeah sure. Soon as I find my cape."

Majors was tying his sneakers as the police cruiser pulled onto the road and started toward the beaches. Steve hit the siren and accelerated, passing already building Saturday tourist traffic.

"What's the hurry? Roger told me that someone has already bought it."

Steve hesitated a moment then uncomfortably spoke up, "There's something I didn't tell Roger."

"Yeah, what's that?"

The deputy removed his hat and placed it on the seat between them. He slowed for a curve in the road then as he accelerated once again with a clear road ahead, turned to Majors, "It's your boy."

Majors started and sat up quickly. "Oh god! No!"

"No, no!" Steve quickly corrected, feeling foolish for being so imprecise. "The boy's okay. He's alright."

Majors regained control of his emotions though his heart still retained its rapid pace. "You mean, Blacky." He honestly didn't want an answer.

"Yeah. I think so," Steve replied, uncertain.

"You think so," Majors returned quickly. "What do you mean, 'you think so'?"

"Well, the call was kind of vague. But the boy is fine. I made sure of that."

Majors sat silent, staring apprehensively down the road.

"We'll find out more in a minute," stated Steve as he slowed to turn onto the beach access.

Majors was out of the cruiser before it came to a full stop just short of a small crowd forming around a red pickup truck with a white cross on the door. Its lifeguard driver was replacing a torpedo buoy on a rack on the side of the vehicle when Majors grabbed the deeply tanned young man and spun him around. The lifeguard's eyes rounded with surprise.

"Where's the kid!" demanded Majors.

Before the lifeguard could respond, Steve took Majors by the arm, "Over there. In the Marine patrol car," he pointed.

Majors pushed his way through the crowd until he came to see his son sitting alone on the rear seat. He paused, relieved the boy was alive and obviously healthy. Opening the vehicle door, Tony looked up and immediately went to his father's arms. After a silent moment he began to cry.

"It's alright, son." Majors could think of nothing else to say. He simply held his son securely. The boy was trembling in tears, his father sure he could feel the sadness his son was feeling. He said nothing until finally Tony spoke.

"He's gone, dad. He's gone."

"Who's gone, son?" Majors asked, searching the boy's eyes. "What happened?"

"Blacky. He just disappeared! He's gone!"

"Are you okay?"

Tony shook his head yes as he sat back on the seat of the car.

"I'll be right back," Majors told the boy. "Are you sure you're alright?"

Tony nodded once again.

Majors looked through the crowd for a source of information. He spied Steve conversing with a Marine patrolman and a heavily tanned and wrinkled old man wearing nothing but a skimpy black bathing suit. He made his way to the trio and placing a hand on Steve's shoulder, asked what had happened.

"This is the boy's father, Frank Majors," Steve informed the two men. "Frank, this is Lance Harvey and Paps."

Major's eyes went desperately from one to the other as they were introduced, "What happened here?" he repeated.

"Well Paps here says he saw the whole thing," said Harvey, the Marine Patrolman. "Says he was in the dunes up there with his binoculars."

"That's right," injected the old man. "I was eatin' breakfast, hard-boiled eggs and a beer, and watchin' some dolphins playin' 'round out there past the surf line."

Majors recognized the old man. He had seen him wondering up and down the beach many times searching for whatever with a metal detector. It seemed mostly tourist and old folks used them. Paps was a regular fixture.

"The kid there," Paps gestured toward the car where Tony sat quietly, "and Blacky... I knew Blacky, ya know. Saved my life once. He was a good boy. They were the only ones on the beach. Except for me of course. Well Blacky was in the water on a surfboard and the kid was on the beach. Well, one minute he was there and the next he wasn't, ya know?" The old man looked out to the surf and jiggled his hand monkey like.

"What do you mean?" asked Majors.

"Well, he just kinda' went under. Kinda' flipped over and under."

"He get caught in a rip," Steve asked Harvey.

Harvey shrugged, "Not likely. Especially Blacky. He was a lifeguard right here on this beach for three years."

"That's right," injected Paps. "That's when he saved my life. Couple a summers ago. Really strange."

"What's strange?" asked Majors.

"Blacky. He went under, board and all," clarified Paps. "And ya know them things just don't sink."

Majors and Steve exchanged a quizzical glance.

"No one recovered the board?" asked Steve.

"Found a piece of it," answered Harvey. "The back part with the skeg." he stated as he pointed to the lifeguard's pickup where the portion of the board lay glistening in the sun atop the hood.

A woman tourist said something about how terrible it all was. "Oh my," she repeated to his sister. "Oh my. This is so sad. A young boy is dead. Oh hun. Oh my." It was her Baltimore accent that made her stand out in the crowd.

Then a couple of blond headed bubba boys mingled through the crowd pronouncing loudly, "Ya'll better watch out! Jaws' gonna' git ya!"

Harvey grabbed one of the boys by the arm, squeezing it tightly, "You boys get the hell outa' here before I kick your asses all the way to your daddy's barbecue shack."

"Shi-it, Stony," one boy replied, "Ya'll don't own the beach."

Harvey stared harshly at the boy, squeezing his arm even tighter. The boys understood he meant business and turned away. As they made their exit down the beach they began to proclaim the presence of the famous killer shark once again.

Majors turned to Paps, "What did my boy do when all this happened?"

"Shoot, when I saw what happened I ran down to the beach. By then your boy was makin' his way through the breakers screamin' for Blacky. Well, I grabbed him. You got a strong kid there mister. He got away from me twice. Tryin' to get out there in the deep water after Blacky. Screamed himself hoarse, he did. But Blacky was gone."

Majors looked back to his son, visualizing the scene that took place. James "Blacky" Blackburn was family. The boy had to be feeling a terrible emptiness and emotional pain.

"Steve, I'd like to take Tony home."

"You think maybe we should stop by the hospital first?" suggested Steve.

"No, just home." Majors turned to the old man, "Thanks Paps."

The old man winked acknowledgment as Majors turned away and walked to the patrol car where he leaned to the window, "Get your board son. Let's go home."

Tony looked up to his father, his eyes still filled with tears, leaving Majors to wonder how long it would take for the emotional pain to leave him or at least resign itself to the farther recesses of his soul.

Chapter Three

"**G**ood morning Captain."

Elliot froze at the sound of the voice on the phone.

"Captain Elliot, are you there?"

"Yes."

"Well then, how are you this morning, Captain?"

Elliot knew this was no mere social call. The man on the other end of the line was not supposed to contact him. This was his rule, not Elliot's. And to contact him when he was on duty meant something had gone seriously wrong. Elliot became uneasy. He thought his obligations to this man were complete.

"I'm fine," he replied carefully after a moment of hesitation. "And yourself?"

"Very well, thank you. Though I've had a business setback recently. Nothing that cannot be corrected, I'm sure. I'm in town for a short time, Captain, and thought it would be nice if we got together. Maybe a little outing. We could discuss my business problem."

Elliot knew he couldn't refuse, but offered no reply.

"Well Captain? What do you say?"

Still, Elliot said nothing.

"My man will pick you up at your home around six. We will have dinner on board the Raven. I'll see you tonight then, Captain Elliot."

With that the phone went dead but Elliot's thoughts had already begun to race through a multitude of questions. He barely heard the click and buzz from the other end of the line. Something had gone wrong, he thought, very wrong. Could it be traced to him? Was it something he did or didn't do? What, damnit, what!

Captain Arthur C. Elliot had left the office early, claiming he was feeling ill. Now and for the past few hours he was pacing the length of the sun porch of his home overlooking the beach a short distance from the Naval Base at Mayport. It was at Mayport where Elliot has been involved for the past two years in an intensive research program. A program conceived by him and involving a small select group of civilian and military personnel, the concept of which was the creation and development of a cost-efficient system for retrieving equipment, test hardware, and whatever else the Navy decided to throw into the sea and wanted returned. Elliot and his team had created for this purpose an unmanned self-propelled computerized submarine system that required no tethering or control. As an added bonus they also created a computerized guidance system much like that of a missile but which worked extremely well underwater. It was developed and applied to a new jet propelled torpedo, or submersible missile as it was labeled, and became a complimenting addition to the Dolphin Retriever, Elliot's primary project.

In Elliot's opinion the program was going well. His schedule for development had been followed; research and development test successful, and few problems had altered their progress. The Navy, though excited about and quickly accepting the system, was pressing and complaining about cost and time. Elliot was annoyed at this and the fact that his labor would most likely result in a mere commendation and a pat on the back for him but a very lucrative contract for a civilian or possibly a former Navy man who had the good sense to put his talents to work on the outside. It annoyed him so much that he sold the system, his system, to the man on the phone. The money was good and he had been satisfied he deserved it. Now something was wrong. For the first time he doubted his decision and with that doubt came fear.

The doorbell rang. Elliot checked his watch. It was six o'clock exactly.

"An excellent dinner, Captain. Do you agree?"

The man used the title of Captain as though it were Elliot's proper name. Elliot was sure it was to remind him of his status as a traitor.

"Yes, excellent," Elliot replied.

"You've been reserved all evening, Captain. No need really."

"Why did you contact me?" Elliot asked bluntly. "We both agreed…"

"Please Captain, don't get excited. As I mentioned over the phone, we have a small problem. Simply a technical problem, I'm sure."

"The Dolphin works perfectly. I tested it myself. Your people are trained. You should have no problems at all," Elliot defended.

"You are quite correct, Captain. The Dolphin works well. It does what it is designed to do. Perhaps too well."

"I don't understand."

"Let's retire to the deck. What are you drinking?"

Elliot rose simultaneously with his host, "Scotch. Straight." He was tense, though he'd been drinking steadily after arriving home earlier that evening.

His host disapproved of Elliot's choice but motioned the steward to fill the order just the same. "You should consider an after dinner wine, Captain.   More pleasing and less intoxicating. Provided you consume it in reasonable quantity, of course."

They strolled the deck of the classic old Trumpy yacht, Elliot enduring the trivial conversation of the man he thought he could not like under any circumstances. A man who was obviously wealthy, had no revealing accent and was always proper in manner and attire. A perfect host and a perfect mystery. First impression left Elliot with the conclusion he was *old money New England.* It was all there, all apparent, all but the name, *Whitemoon.* He was six feet exactly with light brown hair, dark sunned skin and completely expressionless hazel eyes. Considering his age, somewhere in the mid fifties Elliot guessed, his physical condition appeared to be as perfect as his lifestyle. It was all of this that made Elliot uncomfortable, this plus the man's confidence and power. He projected the kind of assumed power that one never questioned, that of a man who never compromised and never lost.

Reinforced by another Scotch, Elliot paused and turned, "Why am I here?" he interrupted Whitemoon. "What the hell is the problem?"

Whitemoon, without breaking stride or reacting to the interruption, finished his comment about his favorite wine, then as though it were part of the conversation, said,
"Your Dolphin, Captain, is a killer."

"That's ridiculous," replied Elliot, laughing nervously. "Completely ridiculous. What the hell are you talking about?"

"Early yesterday morning your Dolphin retrieved a man instead of the sub container. Naturally this man, whoever he was, is dead."

"That's crazy!" Elliot replied angrily. "It's impossible."

"It would seem so. Just the same it happened, Captain. Like it or not, it happened."

Elliot finished off his scotch and turned to the open sea hoping to hide his face that he knew must have paled with Whitemoon's revelation.

"It's impossible," he declared once again. "Your people must have screwed up."

"The Dolphin has been checked out completely, Captain, and it functions perfectly as you say. However there must be a defect somewhere in the system. I agree, it does seem impossible that it could home in on a living object and retrieve..."

"A man."

"Pardon?" questioned the interrupted Whitemoon.

"A man, damnit! It grabbed a man, not an object."

"Really, Captain. You're a career military officer. You surely aren't concerned about the life of a worthless surfer."

"Surfer?" Elliot turned back quickly.

"Yes."

"Did the Dolphin retrieve the board?"

"Part of it, yes."

"I have to see it," Elliot demanded. "Where is it?"

Whitemoon paused considerably, looking deep into Elliot's eyes. "Is it necessary?" he questioned.

"Yes," replied Elliot. "If you want answers that is."

"Needless to say, Captain Elliot, the crew handling the Dolphin was quite upset. Since I was still in the area I had the... remains... transferred aboard the Raven. This constitutes tremendous unnecessary risk not to mention the unsavory inconvenience. Make your observations, Captain, and then correct the problem. I can not afford any further delays and I want that... mess, off this boat before we dock tonight."

Whitemoon raised his hand and motioned quickly. A tall solemn crewman stepped out of a dark passageway startling Elliot who hadn't been aware of anyone's presence other than Whitemoon and himself.

"Take the Captain below. He would like to examine our cargo," Whitemoon instructed the crewman.

"This way, sir," the crewman complied.

Elliot followed, wondering why his host chose not to accompany them. He was taken to a walk-in freezer below decks where the crewman paused at the door and motioned for him to enter. Elliot hesitated, then opened the heavy insulated door. As he did, the crewman reached over his shoulder and switched on the light. Elliot immediately focused on a large object covered with a plastic tarp lying in the center of the floor of the freezer.

"Is that it?" he inquired.

The crewman simply smiled sadistically as he stepped past him and removed the plastic cover.

Elliot felt his stomach tighten. He fought the sickness with all his will, not wanting to appear weak in front of Whitemoon's man and certainly not desiring to give the man any satisfaction by reacting as he expected. Suddenly he found himself regretting his choice of after dinner drink.

Under the plastic cover lay Blacky's broken and mangled gray body and the remaining portions of his surfboard. Though the body was frozen, Elliot could smell the death, an odor that would remain with him in memory to stimulate his guilt.

Chapter Four

The Washington, D.C. traffic was typical, not bumper to bumper but confused by the combination of local population wanting to get somewhere fast and the aimless and careful wondering driving of foreign and American tourists. The cab driver mumbled something about the mall being a damn circus and impossible to drive this time of day. His passenger however was concentrating on the contents of his briefcase, paying little attention to the cabbies disgruntled remarks.

"You don't look like a tourist. You work for the museum?"

"What?" the distinguished middle-aged black man in the back seat looked up. He hated cab drivers, barbers and any stranger in general who asked questions for the sake of small talk courtesy or rude curiosity. It reminded him of the hustlers on the streets of his hometown, Detroit. The way they'd pick your brain and size you up before they hustled you out of everything but your shorts.

"I said, you work for the Smithsonian?"

"Oh, no. Just doing some research," he lied, then gazed out the window hoping the driver would accept his brief statement and pay more attention to his task.

"Sounds cool," continued the cabbie. "You into history and stuff like that?"

The passenger, John Cannon, sat silent. Damn cabbies ought to work for the CIA, he thought, mothers always asking questions. "Just drop me here," he stated coldly.

"You're stop's just down the street. Just take a minute."

"That's okay, I'll walk."

"Don't blame ya. Probably be faster anyhow," agreed the cabby as he brought his vehicle to a halt without pulling over to the side of the street.

Cannon exited the cab quickly, paid the cabbie and started walking toward the Smithsonian Museum of Natural History. Upon arrival he had to make his way through a group of school children that were seated haphazardly about the many steps at the front entrance of the building, then entered, passing a guard who apparently did nothing but count visitors with some little clicker gadget in his hand. A hell of a way to make a living, thought Cannon. Another token federal job for another token citizen but hell, better than welfare, he concluded. Better than the humiliation of welfare he had to endure as a youth.

He continued through the lobby to the part of the building containing the African culture displays and once arriving began to stroll casually. His interest was directed more in the people around him than the exhibits. He rounded a corner near the end of the corridor that opened to a larger room introducing the ice age where he noticed an elderly man in a gray three piece suit gazing pleasantly at a life size statue of an African warrior. He walked slowly to the gentleman's side. For a moment neither man acknowledged the other's presence until the older gentleman finally broke the silence when he stated without turning, "It's called *Defiance*. A perfect title and description for such a piece."

"Indeed," agreed Cannon.

"Or perhaps it should be *Proud Defiance*, Mr. Cannon," the gentleman suggested. "The pride of strength is so profound."

Cannon offered no reply. He simply gazed at the statue, soaking in the power reflected in the muscular form and the defiant angry expression of the face. Have we changed so much, he wondered? He had seen this posture and this expression before, mostly in the sixties when he and many others challenged the nation. He then wondered why his contact chose to meet him at this particular spot with this particular statue. Was it an insult or a compliment or, as Canon suspected, did the gentleman really appreciate it for what it was, a truly moving piece of work.

"You're late, Mr. Cannon," the gentleman stated, continuing to appreciating the statue.

"My flight was late."

"I understand," accepted the gentleman.

From top to bottom, the elderly man oozed with educated dignity. He was wealthy and equally influential. Cannon was not sure of the extent of the man's influence though he did know he and his associates manipulated events throughout the world and power of that magnitude was not to be dealt with lightly. Cannon served them and they paid him well. It was a neat arrangement, clear-cut and simple. You did what they wanted you to do and they rewarded you well. Should you fail or refuse they killed you. This was not some obscure understanding but a clearly stated and proven fact.

The Committee, as they called themselves, was defined and precise in its methods and purpose. It functioned without personality and often without explanation. It expected total dedication and loyalty, full consideration, and took great measures to insure each member and servant remained within their limits. Each individual knew only one person above him and that person was nameless. The elderly gentleman Cannon was meeting with now was his personal nameless key to the higher world of the Committee. To Cannon, the committee was only a name that somehow hovered sightlessly above the world. Like the old Sunday school tales of God, the committee was omnipresent and like God, thought an agnostic Cannon, there was great suffering to justify the goals of the Committee, not the needs or goals of the suffering masses.

"Let's walk, Mr. Cannon."

They strolled slowly through the museum, occasionally pausing to observe various exhibits, bringing Cannon to become restless. He tolerated the man's interest and occasional observations leading him to believe the gentleman was probably more knowledgeable than the museum staff and certainly more appreciative of the past cultures he was observing. A definite conflict of the Committee's purpose, thought Cannon. He wondered if the Committee thought the same or if this man was indeed part of the Committee. He quickly dismissed the thought.

"We may loose all of this, Mr. Cannon. Assuredly, we will loose a great deal."

"It can't be avoided?" questioned Cannon, regretfully.

"No, I suppose not," the elderly man stated sadly. "I suppose not."

A small girl moved in front of them and paused to observe a display of natives in their natural environment.

"It's for them, Mr. Cannon," he said, gesturing to the little girl. "We must realize this. We have to realize this."

"If they survive," said Cannon dryly.

"Let's get down to business. We both have work to do," the older man stated, his mood changing with Cannon's comment. "The Committee is interested in the progress of Whitemoon."

"He's moving along well," reported Cannon. "He's following his schedule accurately but seems to have slowed a bit on his final installation."

"That would be the one near Jacksonville?"

"Yes, the old Naval air station at Green Cove Springs. He's feeding it through St. Augustine."

"What seems to be the problem?"

"None that we can find but he met with his Navy man yesterday. It's possible he may have had a problem with the Dolphin."

"Dolphin?"

"It's a system the Navy developed to retrieve equipment from the bottom of the sea."

"Interesting. What could Whitemoon need with such a system?" questioned the gentleman as he followed the progress of the little girl.

"Apparently Whitemoon's funds have become limited. He has sold much of his business interests and is using the system to smuggle drugs into the country to finance his operation. I have it all here in my report," said Cannon.

"The man is very resourceful. I admire him. His is... an intelligent insanity."

They continued down the corridor toward the center of the museum. "He must not fail. We will have to somehow filter funds in to support him, Mr. Cannon. It's essential that he does not fail."

"I've taken care of that. We're buying all the drugs he brings in. We're even overpaying for them."

"Excellent. I commend you, Mr. Cannon. Very good indeed." They paused once more before entering the lobby of the museum entrance. "Now, what is becoming of the drugs? I do not want them on the streets."

Cannon hesitated. He seemed worried.

"Is something wrong?" questioned the man.

"Not any more," Cannon said as he eyed the guard who was still counting the visitors who entered the museum. "We lost one of our agents. Something went wrong. He soured on us so we set him up as a drug dealer and made sure he was killed by the police during the bust."

"Can he be linked to us?"

"No."

"We can not be tied to this in the event of Whitemoon's failure. That's paramount. You understand that of course?"

"Yes."

"Our work begins only after Whitemoon's operation is completed and, of course, Whitemoon must never learn of our existence."

"I understand." acknowledged Cannon.

"You seem… a bit depressed, Mr. Cannon."

Cannon remained silent. It was clearly understood he was not to question either the means or the ends but it was equally clear he was troubled about both.

"They brought it on themselves. Change does not come easily."

"Does it have to be so destructive?" asked Cannon sincerely.

"You should know better than I, Mr. Cannon. We followed you through the turmoil of the sixties. Your people won their pride but what else did they win? Despite your peaceful effort and that of your other leaders your people have no more than they started with. Our ends will justify our means and regardless of the massive cost and destruction the barriers and borders of this world will finally be dissolved. This planet will become one nation, Mr. Cannon, one great society. This is not some idealistic dream. We are making it happen. *You* are making it happen."

They paused in silence. Cannon removed a heavy brown envelope from his briefcase and passed it to his contact.

"Good day, Mr. Cannon," the gentleman said as he received the report. "Have a most pleasant flight."

Cannon quickly exited the museum, inhaling deeply as the cool air of spring engulfed him, seeming to lighten him, to relieve him of the intense reality of the Committee. Though he still believed in the purpose of the Committee, if for no other reason than by default and the elimination of other failed efforts, he sometimes found their means and methods overpowering in scale and concept. Sometimes to such a degree he found his thoughts swimming in a sea of confusion, nearly suffocating.

Having more than four hours before his return flight, he decided to walk the mall. On a nearby park bench an old black man lay with a newspaper over his face. Further along the mall some children played catch with a football, some people were reading, some picnicking, others jogging. At the far end of the mall, beyond the Smithsonian buildings and other landmarks, he viewed the United States Capitol building. It was larger, seemingly more majestic than he remembered. Perhaps because the last time he was here he was surrounded by thousands of African Americans and he was concerned only with the issues of his people.

Soon this will all be gone, he thought, and there will be new cities in a new world.

Chapter Five

"**W**ho is he?"

"You mean, who *was* he?"

"Alright, if you want to be technical. Who *was* he and *what* was he?"

"*What* he was, was a drug dealer. *What* he is, is dead. *Who* he was before he got dead, we don't know."

"Are you telling me, after I came all the way from D.C. to look at a corpse that you don't know who the hell he was."

"Easy, General. I didn't ask you to come down here."

"I'm not a damn General and someone here sure as hell got the Navy all excited about something."

"Hey man, listen. I'm just a local fuzz, General. All I did was pass on the info. I passed it on to my boss and my boss passed it on to your boss and…"

"Okay fine. Now, Sergeant…"

"Clayton. Deputy Clayton."

"Deputy Clayton, are we finished here?"

"Yeah. Unless you want to look him over completely."

"Now why should I do that?"

"Well, aside from the assorted needle marks and bullet holes, he has the markings of an ex-Navy man."

"The Navy doesn't brand its personnel, Clayton."

"Don't have to. You know, *Mom, Rose, Singapore*. Shit like that."

"Are you referring to the age old sailor's tradition known as tattooing?"

"That's right, General. Looky here." Deputy Clayton lifted the sheet revealing the dead man's outer thigh. "Roll him over."

"I don't do roll over, Clayton," replied an irritated Commander Ramsey Lightner. "You get the big bucks, you roll him over."

Clayton hesitated, clumsily put on a pair of surgical gloves, then abruptly grabbed the right leg of the corpse and raised it enough to reveal the tattoo. "There. Ya see there. He's got an anchor on his ass. Can ya read it?"

"Read what?" Commander Lightner was by this time quite irritated with the deputy and his lack of respect for both him and the corpse.

"The tattoo, damnit. Right there, see?" said Clayton, poking the mark in question with his index finger. "Says right there under the anchor, FTN. That means, *Fuck the Navy*."

"You're a natural born detective, Clayton. Can't say I would have looked there myself."

"Shit," the deputy exclaimed, dropping the heavy corpse back to its original position.

"Okay, so the man may have been in the Navy or maybe he just liked sailors. I didn't fly all the way down here to watch you poke the ass of a dead man. I was told this might be important. So what the hell is so important?"

"Okay, General, okay. Seems Tinker Bell here was into a lot of dope big time. We busted him, or tried to, when he decided to have an old fashioned shoot'em-up but he's the one who got shot up. Or should I say shot down."

"I can see that."

"Yeah, well, before he died he started babbling about missiles. Something about missiles."

"Missiles?"

"Yeah, missiles. Then he started laughing. I think he was strung out. He kept laughing and saying that 'Whitemoon's gonna' get ya, and he thanked us for killing him. Can you imagine that, he thanked us."

"Did he say anything else?"

"That's about it. Just kept laughing and saying, 'Whitemoon's gonna' get us all and there's no place to hide'."

"Did anyone write down what he said?"

"Well, yeah. It's all a matter of record. I'll see that you get a copy."

"Will you let me know as soon as you have an I.D. on him?"

"Well, actually, it's not my bag any more but I'll pass on the request."

"You do that."

"Anything you say, General."

"Clayton, there are no generals in the Navy."

"No shit? Could have swore I saw some Generals in Nam when I was in the Navy."

Commander Ramsey Lightner departed the morgue almost as bewildered as when he had arrived. He was tired with bloodshot eyes and a growing headache, the result, he was sure, of having to take the red eye flight. He had little notice on this assignment and no time for breakfast. His weekend had been ruined by an assignment that in his opinion he and Ma Bell could have handled in ten minutes with long distance ease. Christ! I forgot to call Carol, he thought. She won't understand. She never does. He began looking for a telephone, better yet, a restaurant with a telephone and a good steak when his driver interrupted his search.

"Have you finished here, sir?"

"What?"

"If you're through here, sir, I'm to drive you to Mayport for a briefing."

"A briefing?"

"Yes sir. Captains Downs office."

"Damn." Ramsey's stomach growled. The Navy could wait, he decided. "Is there a good steak house between here and that briefing, Seaman?"

The driver smiled, "That depends, sir."

"Depends? On what?"

"On who's buyin', sir."

"I'll buy, my man. Let's fly," Ramsey smiled in return.

"You got it, sir," stated the Seaman as he enthusiastically opened the door for his passenger.

Thirty minutes later Ramsey sat quietly in a restaurant consuming a steak dinner and trying not to show disappointment in his driver's choice of eating establishment. It turned out to be a down-to-earth place founded only three weeks earlier by some not so down-to-earth New Yorkers. The food was passable, the prices too high and the service made one feel as though they were doing you a big favor. He could have been sitting in a cozy little Italian restaurant with Carol now if it weren't for Peters. Son of a bitch did it to me again, he thought as he chomped vengefully on a large cut of over-cooked steak.

Admiral Elvin J. Peters was Ramsey's superior. He gave out assignments and headaches with very little consideration for anyone's convenience or personal affairs. This was not the first time Peters had put a crimp in Ramsey's love life. Not that his relationship with Carol was that serious but it did require some orderly tending. She was a handful in every way and well worth the effort. He considered her a bonus, one of the only bright lights of experience he'd had in the dark fog of the inner beltway.

As a young man in Evansville, Indiana, Ramsey impatiently studied and planned for the day when he would enter government service and reside among the great honorable men who lived and breathed justice and democracy. He gained his degree in Political Science at the height of the Vietnam War and his commission by way of the reserve officer training deal then served a year at the Pentagon as a legal aid quickly becoming disillusioned with the military justice he had seen, or failed to see. It was then he managed a transfer to combat duty with intelligence in Vietnam and like many others who served with him there, lost his enthusiasm for military service and his faith in human justice in general. Life was simple survival now and honor nothing more than a tactful con for gaining rank and an extended meal ticket. Just the same, with the war ended, Ramsey decided to stay in the Navy and play the game. The security game was easy enough. He worked alone most of the time, avoiding the usual military bull and enjoying the variation of travel. There was also a certain degree of adventure that overshadowed his nightmares of war and civil disillusionment. He often felt and considered himself stuck, uncomfortable with the free wheeling hippie movement and social revolution and quite often equally uncomfortable with the military establishment. He was conditioned for the Navy however, and decided he could better function within its stable environment rather then the ever-changing never lasting civilian circus.

There had been since the war, a void in Ramsey's life that he had difficulty filling. From his college days, even his high school days, female companionship had never been a problem. He found them available and physically satisfying, a pleasant pass time but an obstruction to his career. Now finding them available as before, he would lose interest, feeling one or both of them had reached the limit of sexual and intellectual exchange. Anything further was distracting and time consuming. With Carol came an exception and he wasn't really sure why. Possibly, he thought, because they were of the same persuasion, each expecting little of the other and careful not to give too much. She was colorful and warm, yet she kept her distance. Ramsey was a loner and she accepted this, even admired it. She was however outspoken to the point of shamelessness and quick to anger when it came to any possibility of the type of inconsideration brought about by situations such as the one Ramsey found himself in now.

I have to call her, he thought. Christ! She's got to be pissed off. Probably stomping around Georgetown with that damn college professor. He stopped a waitress and inquired about a telephone then left the driver in mid-sentence.

Three minutes later Ramsey was about to hang up the phone when she answered.

"Speak."

"Carol?"

"Yes."

"It's Ram."

"No shit!" She was obviously angry, more from having to get out of the bathtub to answer the phone than his breaking their date.

"Baby, I'm sorry."

"So what else is new? Where are you this time, Oshkosh or Iran?"

"Will you let me explain?"

"You don't have to. That bastard Peters called. Said you had to leave unexpectedly and didn't have time to call so he thought he would do it for you. That sweet son-of-a-bitch gripes my ass."

"He's just doing his job. I think it was kind of nice of him actually."

"He's a bastard. Look what he did to you last Thanksgiving."

"We made up for that."

"I don't like having to make up. And I don't like long distance love affairs. They're physically impossible. Do you realize I gained five pounds that week? I ate that entire damn turkey. Is that what you want? A fat lover?"

"Carol."

"What?"

"Shut up."

"I can't," she replied, her voice lowering as she dripped water on the oriental carpet.

Ramsey could feel the change, even on the phone. "Why not?"

"Because I'm pissed," she answered. "And I miss you."

There was a pause. Ramsey let it pass. She was cooling off and he knew it.

"Where are you?" she asked.

"Florida."

"How long this time?" she questioned as she sat and began drying her hair.

"I don't know. Maybe a few days, maybe longer."

"I took my vacation today. Two weeks and you're not even here."

"I'll be back."

"When?"

"I don't know."

"I'm coming down there."

"What?"

"I'm coming down. I'm on vacation and I'm going to Florida. How's that?"

"You're crazy." laughed Ramsey.

"No, I'm horny. Where the hell are you?"

Ramsey turned to check on his driver who was now consuming some kind of dessert and checking out the aft end of the waitress.

"I'm in Jacksonville."

"What's in Jacksonville?" asked Carol.

"More Navy," answered Ramsey.

"Where are you staying?"

"Are you serious?"

"Yes, damnit. Now where are you staying?"

"I'm staying at the Sea Turtle Inn on Atlantic Beach."

"The Turtle Inn!" she laughed, "What the hell is a Turtle Inn?"

"It's a hotel, damnit," Ramsey answered, pleasantly irritated. She was in a better mood now. Good or bad, she was always frank and sometimes embarrassing.

"It sounds kind of fruity."

"It's just a hotel."

"Are you staying there alone?" she pried.

"Don't be a smart ass. This is a business trip."

"Bullshit."

"You don't believe me?"

"Of course not." She was working him for an invitation and he knew it.

"See for yourself," he said, giving in.

"I'll see you tonight," she stated quickly then abruptly hung up the phone.

Ramsey laughed to himself, replaced the telephone receiver and returned to his table just in time to pick up the check.

Chapter Six

Ramsey entered Captain F. Edward Downs' office to discover a surprising air of casual clutter and informality, atypical by any Navy standards.

"Commander Ramsey Lightner, sir. Naval Intelligence, Pentagon," he introduced himself.

"Yes, Commander. I've been expecting you. Please come on in and have a seat." Downs' smile was honest and his manner casual, almost to the extent it veiled his wisdom and intellect. "You'll have to excuse the mess. I'm getting out in twenty-seven days and trying to get everything wrapped up before I leave. Not that it matters much. Not a whole hell of a lot going on right now," he chuckled. "I am, what I believe you Vietnam era boys would call, a *short timer*."

Ramsey moved some files from one chair to another then seated himself comfortable. "Twenty-seven days, yes sir, I'd say you're short," he returned.

Captain Downs was searching his desk for something but failed to find it. "Judy!" he yelled to the outer office. "Have you seen my appointment book?"

"Top right-hand drawer, sir," the Seaman clerk responded.

"This is your last meeting today though," she reminded him.

"I know that," he replied, opening the drawer. "The appointment book has my laundry ticket in it."

"No sir," she informed him. "I gave the ticket to your wife this morning." There was an accent of amusement in her voice.

"Oh. Thank you," Downs replied. He looked at Ramsey and smiled, "I'm not senile, Commander. My wife just called and reminded me to pick up my uniforms at the cleaners. She's been very busy lately, distracted. We're moving to our farm in Vermont. I guess she has a lot on her mind. Hell, after thirty years of moving, you'd think she was used to it. Ever been to Vermont?"

"I drove through on the way to Canada once. Beautiful country."

"Yes it is," Downs agreed with a smile as he leaned back in his chair and began cleaning his pipe. "Judy! Where the hell is Eisen?"

"He's on his way, sir," came the voice from the outer office.

Ramsey could see the means of communication between Downs and his secretary was standard play with both of them apparently ignoring what appeared to be a perfectly operable intercom phone system sitting on the old sailor's desk. He found the scene amusing. A pleasant change from the careful intentional atmosphere of Washington.

"I take it you stopped off to visit with our dead man?"

"Yes sir. Though I don't see any urgency in the situation."

"Well maybe not. I didn't either but I felt your people should be notified. I'm old school but I'm no fool. These days when someone says *missiles*, everybody jumps."

An interrupting knock came at the office entrance. It was Eisen.

"Get in here Eisen. Let's get this pow wow over with. I'm on overtime here, ya know. Also have some outstanding pot roast waiting at home."

Eisen entered, glanced at the mess and smiled, "You're not wasting any time are you, sir?"

"Would you, Lieutenant," Downs replied with a chuckle.

"No sir. Guess not."

"Lieutenant, this is Commander Ramsey Lightner, Pentagon."

"Afternoon sir," greeted the young officer, shifting a brown folder to his left hand in order to shake hands with Ramsey.

"He's here to investigate our dead junky missile man," said Downs, finishing the pipe cleaning and tossing the now black cleaners in the trash. "What have we got so far?" he continued, pointing to a cluttered chair for Eisen.

Eisen cleared off the chair, sat and opened the file. "He *is* ex-Navy as the police expected. A Petty Officer Frederick Charles Dillair. Has an excellent record, accelerated promotions, a number of commendations while serving in Vietnam. Entered the Navy in sixty-eight, was a radar technician, got into missile launch control. He applied for officer training in seventy-seven, was accepted but then applied for a hardship discharge soon after. Something about his father dying of cancer. His discharge was approved, and then that's pretty much just about it. We don't have anything on him after that." Eisen flipped through the file and brought out a fresh note, "We checked his home of record. This is a little weird."

"Weird. What?" asked Downs.

"Well sir, his mother says she hasn't seen much of him since he got out of the Navy. She also says the guy's father died in seventy-five of a heart condition, not cancer in seventy-seven."

"Was he married?" asked Ramsey.

"No sir, not that we know of."

"And you have no idea what he's been into since he left the Navy?" asked Downs, packing his pipe.

"No sir. Only that he rented an apartment less then six months ago. Bay Street, Neptune Beach."

"Source of income?" asked Ramsey.

"Told his landlord he was a disabled Veteran with full benefits. Malaria. The previous address he gave was St. Augustine. It didn't check out."

"What was he busted for?" questioned Ramsey.

"Nothing worth dying for. At least I wouldn't think so. The police found a little cocaine and a couple of ounces of pot," answered Lieutenant Eisen. "Although he was a confirmed high volume dealer according to the report."

"And that's all we have?" came Downs.

"That's about it, sir. The police are going to give us an inventory of the items found in his apartment," Eisen concluded, closing the file.

"Not much," said Ramsey. "Makes you wonder though. He was obviously a good career man and highly qualified, not to mention career motivated. He weasels his way out of the Navy, then disappears for years and returns a wasted junky. Doesn't make sense. But then I'm in intelligence not criminal investigation. I wouldn't be the one to know what makes these people tick."

"That's exactly why you're here, Commander," smiled Downs "To make sense of it all. You young'ns shouldn't have any problem. I figure between the two of you, you have about forty years to make some kind of sense out of something we have on this guy."

Ramsey cringed at the idea of a lifetime in the Navy. He always considered his career as temporary, though he had none other in mind. It was just his way of convincing himself he had ultimate control. "What about white moon," he asked. "Is that a street name for a drug of some kind?"

"Don't know, sir. I'll check it out," replied Eisen, making a mental note to do so.

"What kind of missiles was this guy into, Lieutenant," asked Downs.

Eisen opened the file, flipped a page. "Nothing fancy, sir. Shipboard surface to air. He also spent some time with the Marines on shore in Vietnam working with the Hawk STA system."

"Nothing fancy! Damn son, I remember when an airplane drew a crowd and you talk about missiles like they come out of a supermarket," Downs stated, grinning with amusement then changing his expression as he inquired, "Those aren't nukes are they?"

"Surface to air, sir. Primarily for air defense but they could be easily converted to nukes for an airburst. What we'd now call a tactical nuke. A missile's a missile, sir. These are considered short range but still, in the wrong hands, anything can be dangerous."

"Damn things," declared Captain Downs. "Push button war gripes my ass."

Downs revelation caused Eisen and Ramsey to look to each other with a subtle smile as Ramsey asked, "Lieutenant, will you call me when you receive the list of... ah, what's his name?"

"Dillair. Frederick Charles Dillair."

"Right. When you get a list of his goodies give me a call. There might be something there to help us out," concluded Ramsey.

"Yes sir. Should have it today sometime."

"Well gents, I think that should do it for now," stated Captain Downs. "Commander you're free to work out of my office. Request any assistance you need. I'll have copies of everything sent to your office at the Pentagon of course. That should keep Admiral Peters happy. By the way is he still a horses ass?"

Ramsey was thinking of a careful answer when Downs continued.

"By the way, where are you staying? I know you're smart enough not to quarter on base."

"At the Sea Turtle Inn, sir." As he said the name, Ramsey remembered Carol with a half smile.

"Well, if you have no plans, Commander, you're welcome to join my wife and I for a pot roast dinner. My wife may be a little distracted of late but I tell you true, she is one hell of a good cook."

"As a matter of fact I have made plans, sir. But I appreciate the offer."

"Quite alright. I'd only bore you with old Navy tales anyway."

They strolled out of the office and stood by Seaman Judy's desk.

"Sir, your wife called again. Said to remind you to pick up your uniforms," she informed Captain Downs, handing him the note.

"But she's got the... Oh hell, I give up," mumbled Downs as he turned and retired to his office.

Ramsey signed out a Navy vehicle immediately after leaving Captain Downs' office. He wasn't fond of being chauffeured, especially by drivers with poor taste and bad manners. He would rather take the chance of getting lost. Forty minutes later he entered the lobby of the Sea Turtle Inn and went directly to the registration counter. "I'm Commander Lightner. Do I have any messages?"

"Yes sir," smiled the young girl behind the counter. She obviously spent a lot of time on the beach. Her hair was sun bleached and she was well tanned. She turned to find the message and as she did, the strap of her loose fitting top slipped off her shoulder. Ramsey caught a side view of her bra free breast. Good tan. No white at all, he thought. She reminded him of a girl he had met in San Diego a few years back and that in turn reminded him of Carol.

"A Lieutenant Eisen called, sir. Just a few minutes ago actually. He said he would call again," she informed Ramsey as she righted the strap, realizing he must have gotten a good look at her well-formed breast. She smiled seductively then caught herself and quickly glanced to a sun bleached blond surfer type who was impatiently pacing the lobby. Ramsey glanced over and decided the surfer must be waiting for the girl to get off work.

"And," the girl added, "your wife said she would meet you in the lounge. It's just through there," she pointed. Making the statement loudly, as much for her boyfriend's benefit as Ramsey's.

"My what?" questioned Ramsey.

"Your wife, sir. She said, if you were breathing and walking on both legs, to send you directly to the lounge." The girl smiled, her strap fell again and this time she left it down. "Have a nice evening, sir."

"Thank you," replied a confused Ramsey as he turned for the lounge. He deliberately steered a course near the counter girl's waiting boyfriend, looked him in the eyes and giving a slight whistle, stated, "Nice tits."

There were few patrons in the lounge and it was fairly dark, as most lounges tend to be. Ramsey made his way along the bar until his eyes adjusted to the poor lighting. Large windows of tinted glass ran the length of the beach side of the lounge and a few tables along the windows were occupied with people engaged in low-key conversations.

A waitress tapped him on the shoulder, "Sir, um..." she hesitated.

"Yes," Ramsey waited.

"Your, um... Your mother would like you to join her."

"What? My what?" replied Ramsey, surprised.

The waitress was embarrassed. "Your mother, sir," she repeated.

Ramsey searched the lounge and spotted Carol at the darkest table of the far end of the windowed wall. Laughing, he thanked the waitress and started walking to join her. Carol rose to meet him halfway, kissed him heavily before he could say anything then started for the door.

"Where are you going?" asked Ramsey.

"To bed," she stated directly. "Care to join me?"

Ramsey flushed, his red face evident even in the darkness of the lounge. He knew the people at the nearest table must have heard and he was afraid to reply, anticipating Carol's unpredictable response.

"Well, how 'bout it, sailor boy?" she asked, pulling him along.

"What did you say your name was?" questioned Ramsey for the benefit of their audience.

"Must be the uniform,' he heard someone say.

"Let's keep it casual," said Carol. "No names."

Carol entered the hotel room first. Ramsey followed, switching on the lights; which Carol quickly switched off as she closed the door.

"I'm horny," she said softly as she slowly snaked her arms around him.

"Sorry, I'm a married man. The girl at the front desk said so. And my mother is here and besides, I hardly know you."

"Screw your wife and your mother," she whispered.

"You're shameless."

"I'm easy. For you, anyway," she stated in a whisper, sliding her hands down his chest to his belt. They kissed passionately while slowly undressing each other and moving for the bed.

The phone rang.

"Nobody home," she said heavily as they continued groping and disrobing. Ramsey sat on the edge of the bed, tossing her dress to the floor. "Probably little Miss Tits at the front desk," speculated Carol, standing in front of him, her long dirty blond hair and beautifully shaped body reflected in the dim light which filtered through the curtain from the seaside balcony. "I told her you were the best the Navy had to offer."

"Thanks."

"I thought you'd appreciate that," Carol laughed.

Ramsey picked up the bedside telephone receiver, "Hello," he answered as he moved his free hand along the inside of Carol's thigh.

"Sir, this is Lieutenant Eisen. Sorry to bother you."

"Quite all right, Lieutenant," replied Ramsey. "I was just about to... do some reading."

Carol slid to her knees and began slowly kissing the inside of Ramsey's thigh.

"What's up, Lieutenant?" asked Ramsey, smiling as he realized the relevance of what he just said.

"Sir, I've got the list of items found in Dillair's apartment. Nothing much to go on but there was a note from a girl. It reads; *Call me tonight. I haven't seen you in days. I miss you baby. Love, Terry.* Then there's a phone number."

"Did you check the number?" asked Ramsey who was lying down now, his eyes closed in pleasure.

"Yes sir. We traced it to an address in St. Augustine."

Ramsey sat up slightly, retrieved a pen from his pile of clothes by the bed and wrote down the address on the back of a postcard picturing the Sea Turtle Inn. Carol pushed him back to the bed.

"Was there anything else?" he asked.

"No sir. No bank statements or any traceable papers. Just drug paraphernalia, clothes, etc."

"I'll check out the address first thing tomorrow, Lieutenant. Thank you for calling. Have a good evening."

"Thank you, sir. Hope you enjoy your book."

"I'm sure I will. Thank you."

Ramsey replaced the receiver, tossed the pen and postcard to the floor then reached down and pulled Carol to him.

Chapter Seven

"**W**here are we going?"

"St. Augustine."

"What's in St. Augustine?" Carol asked.

She was fixing her hair, using the rear view mirror. Ramsey yanked the mirror back to its original position. He wanted to change lanes and preferred using the mirror rather than looking over his shoulder.

"Why do women do that?" asked an irritated Ramsey.

"Do what?"

"The mirror."

"Vanity, pure vanity. If I'm in a wreck and get killed I want to look my best." She replaced the makeup in her purse, closed it, then placed the purse on the seat between them. "So what's in St. Augustine?" she repeated.

"A lot of history, scenery and tourist traps," answered Ramsey.

"I thought this was a business trip."

"It is."

"Then why the tourist thing?"

"Don't you ever stop asking questions?"

"That's my job, remember. They pay me to punch questions into computers. Day in, day out. It's a habit, like brushing your teeth or having sex."

She fixed her eyes on Ramsey to gage his response. He afforded only a cursory half smile.

"I have to see a girl in St. Augustine."

"Ah huh, I knew it!"

"Wrong, computer wiz. It's not like that," defended Ramsey.

"Sure, tell me about it, spy guy."

"I'm not a spy, for Christ sake."

"So you're going to look up a girl just for old times sake."

"You're a pain in the ass, you know that," he stated flatly.

"But you love it," she smiled teasingly.

"Yeah, I love it," he admitted, patting her on the lap.

Cruising south along the coast road, A1A, they soon found themselves surrounded by palm trees and a host of broad-leafed palmettos and tropical scrub brush. As the palms thinned they were replaced by windblown oaks that had been mysteriously but beautifully mangled and twisted over the years by the constant sea breeze. On the left were huge sand dunes covered with more palmettos, sea oats and scrubs. Further down the road to the right spread an inland lake splattered with small palm islands and alive with cranes, other birds and fish. A few cars were parked on the beach side of the two-lane road. Some were rusty old-model vehicles sporting surfboard racks on their roofs, others were late model family sedans sitting there, clean and shiny, smoldering in the already escalating morning heat.

"What's that?" Carol exclaimed, pointing to a couple of teenage boys behind an old pickup truck on the road shoulder.

Ramsey slowed as they passed. One young man was reaching into a large white canvas sack and as they passed he withdrew a wildly twisting five-foot long rattlesnake. Holding it just below the head, he raised the reptile and, laughing, offered it to Carol for inspection.

"Oh God!" Carol shivered.

The other young man let loose with an assortment of profanities aimed at his companion as he leaped up on the tailgate of the truck, pointing to the ground where the sack had been neglectfully dropped and a second, third, and fourth snakes were finding their way free. Ramsey laughed and goosed the accelerator.

"Oh god, I hate snakes! Did you see that! Oh…" shivered Carol, twisting uncomfortably in her seat.

"Now how can you work in Washington and hate snakes?" questioned Ramsey, seriously. "That city is full of them."

"Don't remind me," she replied. "I'm on vacation, remember. I don't want to think about things like that."

As they drove south approaching St. Augustine an occasional beach house cropped up amid the dunes. Eventually the rustic houses became more frequent, becoming a small beach community.

"What's this?"

"Vilano Beach."

"How'd you know that?"

"I read the sign. If you'd quit messing with the damn mirror you'd see things like that. St. Augustine is just across the bridge there."

When they drove onto the Vilano bridge a bell sounded repeatedly and a long wooden barrier let itself down to stop traffic. Ramsey brought the car to a full stop in front of the flashing red light affixed to the barrier and shut off the engine. He rolled down the window and searched the Intracoastal Waterway for whatever boat the bridge was about to open its large steel expansion for. A few hundred yards south of the bridge a small catch was puttering its way under auxiliary power. On the bridge along the walkway an extremely obese woman sat fishing in a ragged flimsy aluminum lawn chair. Ramsey began calculating the odds of the chair collapsing before they passed on over the bridge. Her children ran excitedly from one side of the bridge to the other, bouncing through cars and dancing from the heat of the asphalt on their bare feet.

"Oh, Ramsey, look!" Carol cried childishly as she opened the door of the car, jumped out and ran to lean over the rail of the bridge.

Ramsey exited the car, slightly embarrassed as he glanced at the occupants of the vehicle behind them. He walked to Carol's side and searched the water in the direction of her excited eyes.

"There! See!" she pointed quickly, her arm stretched out over the rail. "Dolphins! A big one and a baby! A baby!"

Ramsey was now watching Carol, not the dolphins. She gleamed with childish discovery, the sun brightening her blond hair as it separated in the breeze and the reflection off the water enhancing her gray blue eyes. She watched with intensity as the smaller dolphin playfully swam over the back of its mother repeatedly. It was at this moment Ramsey realized he was in love. It had nudged him before when he was with her but he always managed to subdue the feeling. She must have known all along, he thought. That's why she's been so persistent lately and yet knew when to keep her distance.

The dolphins dove deep, avoiding the boat as it cleared the bridge. Carol searched the surface, eventually working her way up to the panoramic beauty of old St. Augustine and the island, Anastasia, joined to it by a distant classic old bridge, the Bridge of Lions.

"Oh Ramsey. It's beautiful. All of it. Look."

He adjusted his view from Carol to take in the surrounding scenery. Sea gulls dipped and glided along the shore where the old city gracefully lined the Matanzas Bay as though it had always been there, before the Spanish arrived in the 16th century, waiting to be discovered. On the western shore of the Bay the old fortress, Castillo de San Marcos, stood soundly, its thick rough coquina walls proclaiming a proud history of defense. Elaborate structures of European-influenced with red tiled roofs from Florida's old wealth and glory days filled the skyline mixed with tall palm trees and smaller buildings sprouting from their original Spanish footprints. On the island, handsome houses with manicured grounds and boat docks rested along the waterfront.

"It is beautiful," Ramsey replied, speaking more of the combination of Carol and this place and the moment.

An irritated tourist laid heavily on his horn and Ramsey quickly realized the bridge had closed and cars were once again moving. He and Carol scurried into the dull blue Navy sedan and flowed with the traffic across to the mainland where a mile later the road turned left, taking them into the town. It was lined with motels, restaurants, fruit stands and countless signs urging tourists to visit here, go there, eat here, take this tour and that. In some ways it took on a carnival atmosphere. The city was historically Spanish and somehow managed to maintain its character but typical shameless, opportunistic American enterprise was abundant.

"I've got to stop and get some directions," Ramsey informed Carol as he pulled into a gas station.

"I thought guys didn't do that."

"Do what?"

"Ask directions."

"We don't. Guys don't, I mean. But the Navy does. How do you think we managed to find Japan and win the war?"

A dark tanned teenager leaning on a gas pump, sweat running down his shirtless chest to heavily soiled jeans, smiled as he adjusted his cap which read *GMC*, to the back of his head. Carol rolled down the car window allowing the heat and smell of gasoline to invade their air-conditioned comfort.

"Yes ma'am," the boy greeted with southern disposition. "What can I do for ya?" His smile revealed poorly maintained teeth and a cheek full of tobacco.

"I'm trying to find Cordova Street," Ramsey stated across the inside of the car.

The boy leaned toward the window eying Carol's breasts. She turned, giving him a better view.

"Yeah, um, well ya go right down there," he pointed toward the inner city. "See them old Spanish city gates across from the fort. Go there an' take a right, then left at the light." He was staring at Carol as he adjusted his chewing tobacco from one cheek to the other.

"Thanks. Appreciate it," Ramsey said as he pulled the car away and checked the traffic for reentry. "Why do you do that?" he questioned Carol, slightly irritated.

A jeep pulling two open-air trams full of gawking tourists moved in front of them and caught a red light. Ramsey would have to wait for the intersection to clear before he could pull out.

"Do what?" Carol laughed.

"You know what."

She rolled up the window and sat back in the seat, "To make you jealous."

"It's not necessary," stated Ramsey as he eyed the tourists seated in the tram. They appeared to be an array of gullible pastel dumplings, dressed in Sears' finest, sitting like a batch of Easter eggs ready to absorb whatever colorful spiel their driver and guide decided to dish out.

"Do you get jealous?" questioned Carol. She was watching a small boy drop the contents of his mother's purse onto the street from the back of the tram. The light changed and the tram pulled off. The wheels of the car behind smashed whatever it was the boy had tossed out and the mother was yet to discover missing.

"Why should I get jealous?" returned Ramsey as he pressed the accelerator. The pale Navy vehicle moved onto the road and cleared the intersection just as the light changed back to red.

"Because you love me?" Carol said with a sly smile.

Not sure what to say, Ramsey drove in silence until they reached the address written on the Sea Turtle Inn postcard. It took him five minutes to find a parking space nearly a full block away from the old gray apartment building, circa 1930, which resembled more a large two story house.

"Why don't you walk around a bit. I won't be long," he suggested to Carol as he exited the car.

"Is she that bad?" she asked sarcastically.

"Business," stated Ramsey.

"Okay, I'll walk. See ya later spy guy," she said as she strolled off toward a souvenir shop.

Ramsey opened the rusted squeaky screen door and entered the dark hall of the old building. A row of small black mailboxes lined the pine-paneled wall. There were no names on the boxes, only numbers. He glanced at the postcard, having to hold it up to a stream of light that filtered through a window next to the door. The place even smelled old, he thought, like another century or the old houses of old relatives you had to visit when you were a small child. Theresa Coggin, he read on the card. Right address, no apartment number. Damn, he thought, he would have to ask around. Behind him was a door on which there was a faded sign stating, *No Soliciting*. "Great, probably a huge damn dog," he mumbled to himself. He knocked on the door and immediately a dog, though much smaller than he had expected by the sound of the bark, began unceasingly to notify everyone in the building of his presence.

"Just a minute," came the weak voice of an old woman from deep in the residence.

He could hear her eventually shuffle her way to the door. When it opened, the dog, a little rat breed he didn't recognize, immediately ran to a back room where it continued its boisterous attack.

"Can I help you?" the woman smiled, half hidden behind the door.

"Yes ma'am. I'm looking for Theresa Coggin. Could you please tell me what apartment she lives in?"

"Well, I don't know. Is she in trouble? She's a nice girl, you know. And if you're selling anything…"

"No ma'am. I'm from the Navy. I just need to talk to her." Ramsey thought the old woman must have failing eyesight. He was in uniform.

"Oh. You must know Freddy. He was in the Navy too. Such a nice boy."

Ramsey assumed she was speaking of the dead junky. If she thought he was a nice boy then he wouldn't argue the point.

"Yes ma'am. I'm trying to find Freddy. I haven't seen him for some time. Just thought I'd stop and say hello."

"Oh yes. Well, he doesn't live here, you know." She opened the door to its full width and glanced over her shoulder then turned to Ramsey secretively, "He comes and visits now and then. Sometimes he spends the night. They think I don't know," she smiled devilishly. "I don't mind. But I don't tell them. Can't let things get out of hand, you know."

The old woman thumbed over her shoulder. Behind her and across the room a much older woman lay motionless in a single bed. She appeared, thought Ramsey, to be dead.

"Mama would never approve, you see."

"Yes ma'am, I understand."

The dog had quieted down and cautiously and fearfully made its way through the apartment, settling under a telephone table. It growled slightly with Ramsey's every move.

Keeping an eye on the dog, Ramsey continued, "If I could speak to Theresa…"

"Oh yes. Um, upstairs. All the way to the back. Now, when you see Freddy you remind him he's supposed to fix my back stairs, okay? He's an excellent carpenter, you know. Fixed my door. Nice boy."

"Yes ma'am. I'll tell him. Thank you." Ramsey turned and started up the narrow staircase. Looking back he noticed the dog had entered the hall and stationed itself at the base of the stairs. The old woman was still standing in the doorway smiling.

There were only three apartments at the top of the stairs. The one at the end of the short dimly lit hall must have been Theresa Coggin's. On the door hung a five by seven inch framed hand sketched caricature with the name Terry D. across the bottom. The sketch revealed a dark haired girl with a dominant smile. Her eyes were large and happy.

Ramsey knocked. Music, Pink Floyd, drifted from behind the door. With the next series of knocks the music was turned off. He waited. After a few silent moments the door finally opened. Sunlight brightly silhouetted the girl as the opening broadened, one hand on the door the other holding a small kitten. She wore a white cotton wrap skirt over a rust colored leotard top. Her facial features were prominently defined, with high cheekbones, full lips and deep brown eyes. Her hair was jet black, complimenting her dark skin but was obviously not original in color. Pleasantly built with distinct muscle posture, she could be a model, thought Ramsey, or an actress.

"I'm Commander Ramsey Lightner," he informed her. "If you're Theresa Coggin, I would like to ask you some questions regarding Frederick Dillair."

She stared emptily at Ramsey. A breeze passed through the open windows of her apartment carrying the mixed scent of incense and marijuana.

"I've been expecting you," she said, standing back from the door. "Please come in."

Her voice, clear and precise, flowed softly, like a sweet heavy cream, thought Ramsey. He was momentarily awed by the first impression thinking for a moment that Freddy, though now dead, was at one time a very lucky man. As he entered her apartment the marijuana scent grew stronger. He saw a glass bong resting on a coffee table in the center of the room. Next to it was a half filled plastic sandwich bag of the pot. She was apparently not concerned the illegal substance was prominently displayed. Around the room hung an assortment of greenery, ferns, spider plants and a few tall floor plants jetted up behind an overstuffed contemporary chair that was covered with an Indian print cloth. Sun streaked in from windows that ran along two walls, more came through the windows of the adjoining kitchen. Smoke lingered in the light.

Moving to the center of the room Ramsey could see more plants in the kitchen and in the bedroom four large marijuana plants grew from clay pots. "You have a very nice place," stated Ramsey, feeling awkward and not sure why.

"Thank you," she replied, seating herself in the Indian print chair. "Please sit down."

Ramsey thought of sitting in the wicker peacock chair across the room but decided it wouldn't gracefully support his six-foot two-inch frame. It also reminded him of some old Bogart movie and he didn't need cloak and dagger visions just now. Instead he crossed to the sofa and seated himself comfortably. He looked at the marijuana then at the girl. She was stoned, he concluded, but hopefully not too high to answer his questions.

Her wrap skirt rose as she adjusted herself in the chair revealing lovely long legs with solid calves. "You're from the Navy?"

"Yes."

"Is Freddy dead?" she asked bluntly.

Ramsey hesitated, "Yes." There followed a long silent uncomfortable moment.

"When?" she asked, focusing her eyes on the kitten that was now busy swatting the low hanging leaf of a corn plant.

"Two days ago. He... he was killed in his apartment."

She didn't seem moved by Ramsey's statement. She knew he was a dealer, he thought. Maybe she expected it. Maybe she was involved.

"He knew something would happen. He was so worried." she said, still showing little emotion.

A strong girl, thought Ramsey, or apathetic, or just plain stoned shitless. "May I ask you some questions?"

She looked to the floor then up to Ramsey, "Yes."

"How long did you know him?"

"Not long." Her focus returned to the kitten. "Um, about six months. We met at the Trade Winds. That's a lounge near the bridge." She began to drift.

"Did you know what he was? I mean, did you know he was a drug dealer?"

"What?" Her eyes lit up slightly and grew with surprise. "He was what?"

Ramsey felt as though he had insulted her in some way. "A dealer," he repeated. "A pusher."

"No... no way. Not Freddy. He hated drugs."

The profile of Fred Dillair began to confuse Ramsey. The man's record was good, the old lady downstairs thought he walked on water and his girl says he hated drugs. "Didn't you know he was a... well, a junky?"

"Are you talking about Fred Dillair?" she asked, becoming as confused as Ramsey.

"Yes, I believe so." He gave her a general description and Dillair's address, then as an afterthought, threw in a description of the tattoo.

"Yes. That's Freddy. But he's no user and definitely not a dealer." She spoke as though he were still alive.

"He was full of drugs when he died, needle marks..."

"No!" she insisted. "I saw him four days ago and I saw his body, all of it, and he never used drugs."

She began to break down. Ramsey caught a slight trembling in her hands and the formation of tears. She collected herself and sat deeper into the chair.

"He... he used to get so upset, even when I smoked pot. Do you know he wouldn't even drink more than one beer in an evening?"

Ramsey had a hard time putting all this together. Either this girl was a fantastic actress or Dillair, the ex-missile man, was set up and killed. He had to start over. "When I got here you said you were expecting me. What did you mean by that?"

She hesitated.

"Why were you expecting me?" he repeated.

"Fred was here four days ago." She seemed unsure that she should continue.

"Yes," urged Ramsey. "What happened?"

"He came late in the night. He was very nervous and didn't look well. I wanted him to eat something and get some sleep. He seemed so worn out. I'd never seen him act so strange, you know? He was always in control and so confident but the other night he lost it completely."

Ramsey sat up with interest. Perhaps something would finally make sense. "What did he say? Did he say anything about missiles?"

"Yes. Yes he did."

She nervously found a pack of cigarettes under a record album on the coffee table, removed one and began searching for a match. Ramsey quickly extracted a lighter from his pocket, lit and extended it. She inhaled then blew the smoke to the center of the room.

"He said something like, 'The missiles were the real thing and he couldn't stop them'. I thought he was having nightmares because of the war or something."

"Yes, he'd been in Vietnam," injected Ramsey. "What else did he say?"

"Well, he was so nervous he even spilled coffee on himself. That's when I got him to take his clothes off and get in bed but he couldn't sleep. He kept rolling around and getting up. He went into the kitchen so I got up and followed him. He was writing something down very fast. He asked for an envelope and I gave him one."

"Did he say anything else?" questioned Ramsey as he scribbled on a small pocket size notebook.

"He kept telling me to go home. Said I would be safer there."

"Where?" asked Ramsey. "Where is home, I mean."

"I'm from Denver."

"Go on," Ramsey insisted. "What else? Did he say anything about a white moon?"

"Yes. Yes, he said, 'Whitemoon was crazy and that I should go home right away'. He looked so pale and tired. I shouldn't have let him leave."

"Where did he go?"

"I don't know. I was asleep when he left."

"He talked about Whitemoon as though it were a person?"

"Yes, I guess so."

"Did he ever mention anyone else?"

"No, not that night."

"Any other time?"

"Um... no."

Ramsey sat quiet for a moment trying to process the facts and put them in order when she interrupted the silence with an additional memory.

"Nikalow."

"What?"

"Nikalow. Fred mentioned someone called Nikalow once."

"When?"

"A few weeks ago. We were leaving the Conch House and he saw a man near his car and..." She stopped abruptly.

"Yes?"

"That's all he said with a tone of concern, 'Nikalow', and we walked on. When we got to the car the man was gone."

"What is it? That Conch place, what is it?"

"What?"

"The Conch House. Is it a restaurant or something?" he repeated.

"Oh, um, it's a little lounge in a marina over on the island."

"Did you and Fred go there often?"

"Yes. Almost every Sunday."

Ramsey thought for a moment. Had he covered everything? Should he dig harder? The girl was getting fuzzy. Maybe he should get back to her later. "Theresa, I may need to talk with you again. Will you be available?"

She remained silent for a moment, gazing across the room at nothing then suddenly the kitten leaped to the coffee table knocking over the bong. She was not affected.

"Um... yes. I work at the Amphitheater on the island or you can reach me here. I do one show a night except on Sunday."

"Show?"

"Cross and Sword. It's a play about St. Augustine. I'm a dancer."

Ramsey stood, placed the notebook in his pocket then reached out and gently took the girl's hand to thank her. She took his hand between both of hers and searched his eyes. If she was lying, he thought, she was a fantastic actress.

He left her a phone number where he could be reached then exited the old apartment building, juggling the information he had obtained around in his mind. Why was she expecting him or someone like him? He would have to speak with her again when she would be less confused and hopefully not stoned. He guessed she would be a fine dancer. A body like that had to be graceful in any situation, he thought, then quickly tried to put the thought out of his mind. Business, Ram, he told himself. Strictly business.

The sound of a rattling carriage and horse hooves on the hard pavement drew Ramsey's attention to the street in front of the old apartment house. A speckled chestnut mare with a broad-brimmed straw hat was lazily pulling a red carriage with a colorful canvas top. Some elderly tourists sat comfortably in the shaded rear as an old black man with a matching straw hat, sprawled sideways in the front holding the reins in one hand and emphasizing his dialogue with the other. He was commenting on the history of an old Huguenot graveyard across the street. Ramsey couldn't understand him fully, something about Christian Indians, a killer plague and local prejudice requiring separate burial locations. As the carriage passed, Ramsey looked across to the graveyard where he saw Carol strolling among the tombstones, pausing now and again to read the worn and faded inscriptions.

The small graveyard was situated behind a three-foot wall of coquina stone with an old iron gate that was closed, chained and locked. He crossed the street to pause by the wall beneath a large oak tree and examine the aged neglected graves. Some were above ground brick boxes that were sagging or had caved in; chains connected to iron posts surrounded others. The tombstones leaned to various degrees, invaded over the years by the expanding roots of the surrounding oaks. Even in a graveyard she was beautiful, he thought as Carol walked through a stream of light filtering through the trees. He wondered why he had never noticed this in Washington, why it seemed different here. He wondered if maybe his session with Theresa Coggin had heightened his perception. Perhaps it was time to leave the city. Perhaps, at age thirty-seven, he wanted a new life.

As the carriage rattled down the street it passed another man paused under the shade of an old oak tree. This man was watching Ramsey and he too was thinking of Washington and graveyards, except his vision of gravestones was massive. Millions of plain white markers without inscriptions extending forever in every direction into and beyond the horizon. He gazed into the future but the vision didn't affect him. His deep-set eyes hid behind sunglasses as he measured the Navy Commander for a possible future encounter.

Chapter Eight

The sun was at its highest point of the day as it seared the sandy-shelled beach and invading people. Their drugstore chaise lounges, plastic coolers, blankets, radios and Frisbees seemed to compromise the island's natural beauty. That along with the smell of cocoa butter and other exotic tanning solutions lingering in the hot air mixing with the odor of salt water and decaying marine life. The tourists wandered aimlessly marveling at the innumerable shells and assorted unidentifiable but beautiful bits of ocean trash that was deposited on the beach by the outgoing tide. All things considered, it was a normal day on the Conch Island beach.

The marine patrol car made its way slowly and steadily along the wide beach and was generally ignored by children who were hastily building sand castles and masochistically waiting for the surf to roll in and pound both them and their sand structures into a joyful wet mess. Nor was it noticed by the tourists, or *pilgrims* as the locals called them, while they braved the small breakers by bracing themselves headlong into the surf only to be easily pushed aside like pesky children by an indifferent ocean. Lance Harvey, better known as

Stony, rested his left hand on the bottom of the steering wheel, his right arm stretched across the back of the seat. He sat poised officially in the cruiser, appearing bored but cool in the gentle steady blow of the vehicle's air conditioning. Finding the least occupied area of the beach, he brought the cruiser to a stop, turned and backed slowly toward the dunes until he reached the edge of the hard-pack sand where the vehicle could sit without getting stuck, then shifted to park, leaving the engine to idle in order to continue the comfort of air-conditioning.

He eased back and relaxed, nursing a cup of ice water until only the ice remained then began to crunch the ice as though it were peanuts. Assuring himself there were no other officials of any kind in the area he place the cup on the seat and extracted a pair of binoculars from the glove compartment, wiped the lenses clean with a napkin then raised the glasses to his eyes. Adjusting the focus, a trawler came clear from a few miles off shore. The boat with nets extended, forged slowly and heavily through the water. After running a mile south along the island coast it swung wide to port and retraced its path north. He watched as the trawler repeated the move again and again, never leaving the one-mile area. Harvey thought it odd. Though he had seen shrimpers run this way before they usually worked a larger area, gradually making way north or south.

The boat slowed as it pulled in its nets. He massaged his eyes, waited for the strain to ease then viewed the boat again. "Empty," he muttered.

After the nets were secured the boat remained in place, a crewman squatting on the foredeck seemed to be searching the water. Harvey watched with intense interest until the crewman suddenly stood and motioned for the attention of the boat's pilot, then pointed to an area in the water about fifty yards from the bow. The crewman then quickly raced aft and disappeared below. Harvey searched the surface surrounding the boat but saw nothing unusual. He massaged his eyes once again thinking he would have to leave soon and decided to give the boat one last look. Raising the glasses and adjusting the focus to his tired eyes he noticed something was different but wasn't' sure what it was. She was underway again, heading north for the inlet. As it reached the end of the island the oddity came to him. She's riding low, he thought, empty nets but now she's riding low. He strained to read the name on the stern but made out only the first four letters as the boat plowed on turning slightly to starboard to maintain deep water. "H A P P... Happy Jack. That's Jack's boat," he said to himself.

Harvey knew Jack Escara well. They had grown up together, fished together and even dated the same girls, playing them like a game when they were both football stars in high school. He hadn't put it together before but Jack has been doing very well lately. A new house on Porpoise Point, a new pickup and of course this new trawler which didn't come for chump change. I'll have to have a talk with ole Jack, thought Harvey. Those boats cost big bucks and his ole buddy was either in debt up to his good ole red neck ass or he was hauling in something besides shrimp. Jack always had something going to gain a buck. What was he into now? Harvey toyed with a strategy of approach, thinking he would check out the boat first then maybe go visit his old buddy or possibly just take a few days off to keep an eye on Jack and see what he was up to. If it was what he expected then he wanted in, he wanted enough money to drop his thankless job and get away from the tourists and heat. He wanted enough money, he thought, to just not have to care about having enough money.

He finished off the ice as he anticipated his approach to Jack Escara and rolled down the window to toss out the cup. When realizing he was being observed by a little boy who had just retrieved an under inflated beach ball, he decided to toss the cup on the floor of his vehicle instead. "Goddamn pilgrims," he mumbled, rolling up the window and putting the car in drive. The vehicle eased out onto the beach where he discovered a van had parked twenty yards away. Four young girls were spreading blankets and setting up aluminum lounge chairs. Harvey slowed to a near stop and smiled, giving a slight wave. One of the girls returned the wave and was nudged by another warningly as she stashed two marijuana joints under a towel. It was one of his favorite scenarios. Caught in the act with dope or boos, he would use their guilt to get in their pants. Most anyone would call it blackmail but Harvey called it *sweet justice*.

He smiled and drove on. You've got bigger fish to fry today, Stony boy, he thought to himself. Much bigger fish.

Chapter Nine

"**I** found a great little place for lunch!" said Carol as Ramsey escorted her across the street.

"Don't you know that when a place has a gate with a lock and chain on it that usually means keep out?"

"It just looked so inviting, so interesting. You know?"

"Yeah, as in, so keep outish."

"It's not like I was going to wake anybody up in there or anything. Now, about that cute little place to eat. I was about to say, I found this great cute little place to eat."

"Is that right?"

"Yes. It's so cute."

"You said that already. I don't like cute food," Ramsey informed her, his mind again sorting the odd interview he had with Theresa Coggin. "And I'm not in the mood for Spanish food," he added.

"It's not Spanish. It's... um. Well, I guess it's Catholic."

"You mean Italian," Ramsey clarified.

"No, I mean Catholic," she repeated. "I guess it's Catholic."

"I've never heard of Catholic food. I don't think there is such a thing."

"This was," she pointed. "There's this street over there, St. George Street, and it's all old Spanish houses and shops. It's so cute."

They turned and walked down a narrow side street toward the city's restoration area soon discovering, as she had described, an old Spanish atmosphere complete with costumed shop keepers, and small buildings of original 17th century design finished in coquina and stucco with overhung balconies and wood and iron fixtures.

"Isn't it cute?" asked Carol.

"Yes," Ramsey conceded. "It's cute, just like Disneyland." He quickly sidestepped to avoid a collision with an ice cream wielding child. Carol recognized the child as the one on the tour tram who had emptied his mother's purse onto the street.

"Little punk," she muttered.

"So, where's the Catholic food place?" asked Ramsey as he regained his balance.

"Right here." She led him through an opening in a waist high wall and into a small restaurant. A young man in a black monk's robe greeted them at the door.

"Welcome to the Monk's Vineyard," he smiled. "Would you like a table or a seat at the bar?"

"Two for lunch," smiled Carol.

The monk swiveled and motioned to a booth near the window. The dining room was small but filled with the atmosphere of a chapel mixed with the décor of a wine cellar. Wooden tables lined the walls and the seating consisted of matching church pews. Wine bottles lined the wood-sash windows and oversized clusters of grapes doubling as lights hung from a latticed ceiling. All in all the place was as Ramsey thought, a little too cute and tacky as hell but it somehow fit just right on old St. George Street and worked like a charm on every tourist that came down the pike.

Carol seated herself and Ramsey slid into the uncomfortable pew across from her.

"Would you like cocktails?" asked the monk waiter, raising a small order pad and pen.

Ramsey winced, turning away to take in the décor. Carol knew what he was thinking and tried to compensate by being cordial.

"Yes," she answered cheerfully. "Amaretto sour for me and a draft for the grouch."

"Yes ma'am. Amaretto and a draft," the waiter repeated as he placed two menus on the table, then turned, flipped his ponytail at Ramsey and strutted effeminately to the bar in the adjoining room.

"Isn't he cute?" Carol nudged across the table at Ramsey who was now reading the menu.

"He's a doll," he stated, not raising his eyes. "I bet his mother is so proud."

"Well, what do you think?" she questioned, opening her menu.

"About the waiter? You know what I think about those damn…"

"No, no. About the restaurant," she clarified. "Isn't it quaint?"

"Yes," Ramsey reluctantly agreed. "It's quaint. That's a better word than cute. The whole town is quaint and the waiter is cute and you're beautiful."

"Shit!" Carol blurted out.

"What, what's wrong?" asked Ramsey, alarmed.

"You," she smiled. "You've never said that before. I love it."

Ramsey wanted to tell her then he loved her. That he wanted a lifetime of unpredictable days and nights with her.

"I need to make a phone call," he said, avoiding his feelings. "I'll be right back."

He walked across the small dining room and tapped one of the other waiters on the shoulder. Carol observed him with the soft grace of a mother eyeing her children. She was quick and observant, rarely missing anything within her range. She knew what he felt and she would let him pick the time, she thought. Time is what she had plenty of. It was her ally.

The waiter pointed to a narrow hall at the corner of the room. Ramsey thanked him and the waiter returned the thanks with a limp wrested gesture. Ramsey gave a disgusted glance across the room to Carol who covered her face with the menu to hide a snicker.

He placed the call to Admiral Peters at the Pentagon. The Admiral had just completed the daily staff briefing and was about to go to lunch.

"Ramsey. How's the land of sunshine?" asked Peters, seating himself comfortably behind the heavy teak desk.

"Very nice, sir. Hot and sunny. Perfect beach weather."

"Good," replied the Admiral. "I didn't think that assignment would turn out to be much. Hell son, take an extra day. If nothing else, you can get yourself a tan before your return."

"Yes sir, if I have time," replied Ramsey, not wanting to leave the impression he would sham while on assignment. "Sir, about this investigation, I need some information."

The Admiral sat up with interest and reached for a pad and pen. His expression turned official, revealing the age lines around his eyes and on his forehead. "What do you need Commander?"

"As you probably know by now, sir, our dead man was ex-Navy."

"Yes. I glanced through the info wired in from Mayport. He was in missiles or something."

"Yes sir." Ramsey shifted the telephone receiver between his ear and shoulder, reaching for his note pad and flipping through to the recent entries from his meeting with Theresa Coggin. "I've got conflicting information here. It seems our man has an excellent military record with a strong technical background in missiles. He abruptly gained release from the

Navy under false pretenses and disappeared for a few years. He surfaced six months ago and spent a lot of time in or around the Jacksonville, St. Augustine area. Now his girlfriend says he was clean as a boy scout but he was killed in a drug bust and found to be pumped up with cocaine." Ramsey paused to review his notes.

"And what girl is this?" asked Peters.

"Theresa Coggin," answered Ramsey. "She's a dancer. Lives in St. Augustine."

"Is she credible?"

"A little flaky but my instincts say yes."

"So you think this man may have been set up?"

"It's possible, sir, but there's no hard evidence, just names."

"Names?" Admiral Peters stopped scribbling on the pad.

"Yes sir. I need them checked out. It may give us some direction. The first is *Whitemoon*. It could be a man's name or an operation of some kind."

"Whitemoon?" Peters set the pad down and leaned back in his chair.

"It's an odd name, sir. I can't connect it with any known operation just off hand however it has something to do with missiles." Ramsey didn't want to get into the desperate condition of Dillair prior to his death. He thought it would convey his over-reaction of the situation to the Admiral and he wasn't going to be the one to push the panic button, not at this point. He was concerned however that Dillair's death, if it were a cover-up, was well executed and most likely involved a great deal of consideration on the part of someone or some organization.

"You need information on Whitemoon?"

"Yes sir. A computer search. Anything at all would be helpful." Ramsey moved close to the wall and hovered over the phone as one of the monk waiters passed on route to the men's room. He continued, "Also need anything on anybody named Nikalow.   Description and name rings Russian or Balkan to me."

"Is that all?"

"One thing more sir. I need to know who we have given the Hawk missile system to during the past three to five years."

"That sounds very serious, Commander.   Possibly international."

"Yes sir, but I haven't got much else to go on."

"I understand. I'll have your request filled and forwarded to Mayport as soon as possible," concluded the Admiral as he crumpled up his notes and tossed them in the trashcan beside his desk.   "By the way Commander, I extended your apologies to Miss Langley.   The least I could do, considering."

Ramsey hesitated, "Um, yes. She told me that. Thank you, sir. I appreciate it." If he only knew, thought Ramsey, that the Navy was footing the bill for Carol's vacation.

"Now, if you don't mind, Commander, I'm overdue for lunch," Peters stated as he rose behind his desk. "I'm dining with General Colburn. Trying to soften that old bastard up so we can use his computers. How he gets the good stuff before we do always amazes me. Can't really complain though. I suppose we get our share. Just a matter of priorities."

"Yes sir," Ramsey agreed, his stomach growling slightly as the aroma of beef teriyaki drifted from the kitchen.

"Don't worry about the info. I'll have Lieutenant Gilmore work it up for you ASAP," said the Admiral as he abruptly discontinued the call by hanging up without any verbal farewell.

Ramsey heard the click and ended his end of the conversation in a like manner.   Typical, he thought, the bastard never says goodbye, just hangs up. Admiral Peters was in good spirits however and that was rare. Ramsey dismissed the thought and returned to his pew where Carol had obtained a local newspaper from somewhere and was musing over the front page when he seated himself. The waiter approached their table with a tray containing two small salads and silver settings.

"I've already ordered," Carol informed him as she slid the newspaper aside.

"Catholic food?" inquired Ramsey jokingly.

"Heavenly Spanish bean soup and the Fryer's Surprise," she replied.

"What's a Fryer's Surprise?"

"I don't know. That's why I ordered it for you instead of myself."

"And what are you having?"

"Beef Teriyaki," she smiled.

Ramsey leaned back, making way for the broad sleeve of the monk's robe as he placed the eating utensils on the table.

"If that Fryer thing isn't good I'm going to eat your teriyaki."

"Baby, you can eat my teriyaki any time," Carol stated seductively.

The waiter cleared his throat as his eyes went to the ceiling in disgust.

"Do you wear anything under that robe?" Carol asked the waiter as she raised the hem of the robe above his knee.

Ramsey, embarrassed, quickly hid his face with the newspaper.

"No ma'am. Much more comfortable this way. Know what I mean?" He tucked the tray under his arm and strutted off.

"Did you have to do that?" Ramsey asked.

"Did you see that?" Carol shot back, laughing.

"See what?"

"His legs. That little… um, monk, shaves his legs."

Ramsey tossed the paper down. "What did you expect?"

"Panty hose," she laughed, looking to see if she had been overheard by anyone.

"You're shameless. But you're amazing," Ramsey retorted. "Let's eat."

"Let's stay here."

"What," came Ramsey through a mouth full of salad.

"Let's spend the night here. Or a week."

"A week!" he gulped. Clearing his throat, he continued. "Carol, this is a business trip. Navy business. I can't spend the week here."

"Why not? Look, there's this big Spanish Days Festival coming up and we could stay at the beach and get some sun. The girls would hate it if I went back to work dark as a native." She played with her salad, eyeing him, anticipating his answer.

Ramsey ate his, ignoring her.

"I look great in a bikini."

"No."

"There's an art festival and Spanish dancers and..."

"No."

"Here. See. It's all right here in the paper," she said as she pushed the newspaper under his nose.

He chewed the salad slowly as he glanced at the front page. The headline read, *Spanish Days Festival To Be Bigger, Better.* "You're impossible," he stated, taking the paper in hand and folding it for ease of handling. By doing so, the bottom fold of the front page faced him and a smaller headline caught his attention. *Recent Drowning Still A Mystery.* He read on.

The recent disappearance of James Blackburn on Saturday, June 14th, continues to baffle local authorities. Blackburn was mysteriously pulled under water Saturday morning while surfing off Conch Island. Howard (Paps) Copeland, who witnessed the incident stated that he saw Blackburn go under the water, failing to surface.

Lance Harvey, a Florida Marine Patrolman who arrived on the scene shortly after the incident, ruled out the possibility of Blackburn being the victim of a rip tide, stating there was no extreme surf or rip tide at the time.

Accompanying Thomas Blackburn on the beach was 10 year old Tony Majors, son of Frank E. Majors, a resident of St. Augustine. The boy's statement coincided with that of Mr. Copeland's. As yet, the unfortunate surfer has not been found and the authorities state the search will most likely continue through tomorrow, ending in the evening.

Ramsey put the paper down and looked at Carol, "Frank Majors, I'll be damned."

"What?"

"Majors is here," stated Ramsey.

"What's a Majors?" questioned Carol as she dissected her salad.

"A friend from the war. He's a journalist. You probably saw him on TV."

"I wouldn't know. They all look alike to me. Did he have his clothes on?"

"You must have seen him. He was very big for a while. On every night during the Mid-East War. A blond headed guy, tall."

"Oh, the one with the microphone?"

"Yeah."

"Nope. Doesn't ring a bell but then I don't watch the news. It's too depressing. And full of bullshit." She was eating her salad now, satisfied she could identify its contents.

"I'm going to call him after lunch. We had some good times together."

"Good. Maybe he can convince you to stay here for a week."

"You never give up do you?" Ramsey stated, raising his beer to his mouth.

"Ham and mincemeat!"

"What?"

"Ham and mincemeat and Swiss cheese on pumpernickel bread," she repeated. "The Fryer's Surprise. It's a grilled sandwich. That's what you're having for lunch."

"No," returned Ramsey. "That's what you're having for lunch. I'm having beef teriyaki."

Chapter Ten

It was late evening when Jack Escara's pickup truck skidded to a halt on the white gravel and oyster shelled parking lot behind the old fish market. There were no other vehicles in the immediate area as he slammed the truck door and made for the dock nearby. He skipped and balanced his lanky body over a pile of old barnacle clad pilings and onto the narrow dock, whistling his favorite country tune as he went. Pausing to light a cigarette, his eyes searched the surrounding dock and nearby trawlers for anyone who may look out of place or locals still hanging around after hours. Not seeing anyone, he continued to the end of the dock where his boat, the Happy Jack, was moored. Kicking a half filled beer can into the water, he long jumped the three-foot distance between the dirty weathered wood planks of the dock and the deck of his boat. Pausing briefly again with the pretense of tying his shoe, he gave the dock area a final surveillance. Satisfied, he then turned and headed for the pilothouse but froze when he eyed a dim light within.

"Damn," he muttered. "Who the fuck..." Escara approached the cabin slowly from the side then braced for whatever or whomever he was about to mix with.

"Hey boy!" a voice blurted from inside the dark pilot house sending Escara back in a start. "Well shit boy. You gonna' stand out there like a dumb ass or you gonna' get in here and have a beer with an old buddy?"

Escara approached the entrance carefully, slowly kicking the door aside. Just as he caught view of the man in the dimly lit cabin something hard flew into his chest. He quickly grabbed at his heart expecting pain or sudden death. Instead he trapped a wet cold can of beer.

"What's the matter boy? You quit drinkin'?" said his unexpected visitor, stepping into view.

"Stony?" said Escara. "That you?"

"Well, shit boy. Come on in. Hell, it's your boat ain't it," Lance Harvey returned through a good ole boy smile.

"Stony... Stony, what the hell are you doin'? You drunk?"

"Nice boat, Jack," Harvey stated as he leaned against a small refrigerator. "Yeah, real nice boat."

Escara moved closer, popping the tab on the beer.

"Long time no see, buddy. You been kinda' busy lately I reckon." stated Harvey.

Escara reached for a switch to turn on the cabin lights.

"Don't bother turnin' on the light there Jack ole boy. I pretty much seen all I need to see."

"What are you talkin' 'bout Stony?" asked Escara as he looked about the cabin for a potential weapon, his eyes settling on a large flashlight nearby.

"Jack, ole buddy, I gotta' hand it to ya. You got one sweet machine here. Musta' cost at least two hundred thousand stripped down. More I reckon. And all them gizmos down there with that underwater thing. Makes a man wonder."

"Stay out of it, Stony. Ain't none of you business," Escara insisted as he seated himself within reach of the flashlight.

"What you catchin' now days, boy? Dope? You bringin' in all that shit that's burnin' the brains outa' this country's fine young children?" Harvey paused, drinking his beer and measuring Escara's reaction.

Escara sat cautiously silent.

"Well, speak up boy. Hell this is old Stony here, remember? I ain't gonna' cut your balls off. This uniform don't make me no cop." Harvey finished off the beer and tossed the empty aside. "Shit boy, you know me better than that."

"Kiss my ass, Stony! You ain't in on this one," said Escara as he stood to challenge Harvey.

Harvey came across the cabin and shot a quick blow to the groin with his foot. Escara let out a painful moan as he doubled over and crashed to the deck.

"I ain't gonna' piss around here boy!" Harvey stated as he knelt beside him. "I want to know how you got this fancy ass boat and what that damn machine is down there. And don't tell me you're doin' marine research or I'll research your goddamn head, understand?" He went to the refrigerator and retrieved another beer. Escara rolled in pain on the floor, his eyes tightly closed, mouth twisted.

"Now listen. You take your time and start at the beginning," he continued, ripping the tab off the can and tossing it. "I got lots of time."

A few minutes later Escara's pain subsided enough to allow him to sit up. He rose and leaned against the table that held the flashlight. "I can't tell you nothin'," he said, holding his groin. "These people don't fuck around. They'll kill you. They'll kill us both!"

"You ain't got no choice, boy. You don't lay it all out and maybe I'll kill you." Harvey boosted himself up on top of the refrigerator, knocking over a few coffee cups and beer cans.

Escara stared in amazement. "Damn Stony. You just don't understand…"

"No! You don't understand!" Harvey jumped from his perch and darted across the cabin facing Escara. "I got your number Jack! I know what you're haulin' and I want my share. You wanta' keep this boat and your pretty woman and that nice beach house over there on Porpoise Point then you better get smart and start layin' names on me. You see, I ain't that greedy. One shot, Jack. Just one shot at those people and I'll be gone with enough money to last one hell of a good time."

"Alright," Escara conceded as he began to rise, grabbing the table for support. "But them people will kill ya, Stoney. Sure as shit, they'll kill ya."

Harvey backed off across the cabin, "Who are they? Where do they…"

Escara snatched the flashlight and attacked, striking at Harvey's head, missing and slamming it into his shoulder. Harvey fell back against the refrigerator, knocking the door open, sending cans of beer toppling out and rolling across the deck. Escara regained his balance and raised his arm to strike again but Harvey dodged the lethal swing by ducking to the deck. He then grabbed one of the cans, rose quickly and smashed it into Escara's face, breaking his nose and splitting the skin beneath his right eye. The can burst and white beer foam, mixed with Escara's blood, sprayed both men and the cabin. Escara's hands went to his face as he screamed and fell. Harvey quickly jammed a knee into his gut, grabbing him by the neck and hair, ignoring the surging pain in his own shoulder.

"Okay mother fucker, start talkin'."

Escara forced the words through the blood as it ran over his face and into his mouth. "Cocaine," he choked. "Uncut. We… we pick it up with the Dolphin off Conch Island."

"Who puts it there?"

"I don't know. I just know when to pick up."

"How much?"

Escara choked. Harvey eased the pressure around his neck. "How much!" he demanded.

"Small containers. Like cigar tubes. They put them in the torpedo."

"How many?"

"Five to six hundred. I pick up once a week."

"Damn!' Harvey exclaimed as he mentally converted the amount of cocaine to dollars. He eased away from Escara and stood across the cabin.

Escara twisted to his side, beer cans rolling as his legs sprawled across the deck.

"How do you move it?" asked Harvey.

"In the fish market," coughed Escara, spitting blood. "In the fish. I stick the tubes in the fish. Some guy picks 'em up."

"Who?"

Escara hesitated.

"Who!" Harvey shouted as he angrily kicked a can of beer across the deck, just missing Escara's head by inches.

"Nikalow. Some foreigner calls himself, Nikalow."

Harvey wiped his face on the sleeve of his shirt, then yanked his shirttail out and wiped it again more thoroughly.

Escara managed to get to his knees, his hands still covering his face, blood running down his forearms.

"What about the money?" Harvey continued.

Escara laughed, even though it was painful, "You wouldn't believe it."

"Try me."

He sat back and looked up at Harvey. "I mail it. I take out ten percent and then I mail it. Nothing like the good ole U.S. Post Office as a partner in crime." His face was swelling to an unrecognizable state. Blood covered his hair and oozed down his neck. "They're gonna' kill you, Stony. Sure as hell they're gonna' kill your ass."

Harvey smiled, "Like you killed that kid on the surfboard with that damn machine?"

Escara's eyes widened with guilt.

Harvey laughed, "Hell boy, surfboards don't sink. I saw your boat out there that day. I didn't know it was you then but I do now. This fancy boat of yours opens its hull and that thing sneaks out, picks up the goodies and sneaks back in. I wish I coulda' seen your face when you opened that thing and found a dead man 'stead of a torpedo." He laughed again as he retrieved another beer from the deck. "Listen boy, next time that Nikalow dude comes around you take care of business as usual, you understand? Then the only U.S. *Male* your gonna' deal with is me. And when they come after you lookin' for their money you just give 'em a phone number. That's all. You got that? Just a phone number."

Escara tried to rise and fell back against the table. Bracing himself, he looked at Harvey, fear crawling over him like slow electricity, "You crazy bastard! You sum'bitch, you're gonna' get us all killed!"

Harvey smiled and finished off his beer.

The following day, still slightly shaken from his encounter with Harvey the evening before, Jack Escara paced nervously behind the glass enclosed fish counter. Also in the market a toothless old man leaning on a live bait tank was revealing his favorite cooking technique for red snapper to a couple of friends. Near the dockside door of the small fish market Lance Harvey rested against the wall in an old chrome and plastic dining chair, his hat pulled down over his eyes, giving the appearance he was asleep. He sat up slowly as a young black boy entered the market with a slam of the screen door.

"Hey, Mr. Jack," the boy greeted.

Escara offered a half smile of acknowledgement.

The boy went directly to a rusty old soda machine and deposited a few coins, pushed his selection and got no results.

"This damn thing broke again, Mr. Jack," the boy yelled over his shoulder.

Escara moved to the cash register, opened it and removed two quarters, tossed them to the boy. The boy inserted the quarters, snatched up the can as it popped out of the machine and stealthily slid the fifteen cents change from the change dispenser into his pocket. Harvey tilted his hat back and stared the boy in the eyes accusingly. The boy looked back to Escara then ran out of the fish market with a slam of the door.

"How come you let that little black bastard get away with that shit, Jack? Came the old man. "Pulls that damn money trick on you most every day."

"He's a good kid," Escara answered, looking uncomfortably at Harvey. "Helps me clean the boat and picks up around here. Hell of a lot more helpful than you, you old fart."

"Sure you ain't got nothin' goin' with the kids mama?" joked the toothless old man.

"How'd you like a red snapper up your ass, old man," threatened Escara as he closed the cash register.

Just then the screen door squeaked open and a tall man with graying hair and goatee entered causing Escara's disposition to suddenly take a turn for the better.

"Mornin' Mr. Nikalow. How's everything in the restaurant business today?" he said with a smile and continued before the man could answer. "Reckon you want the usual assortment. I got it all on ice in the back room. Just hang on here and I'll fetch it for ya."

Nikalow removed his sunglasses, revealing deep-set steel gray eyes that studied the bandage and stitches across Escara's nose and under his right eye.

Realizing Nikalow's scrutiny, Escara explained, "Slipped on the deck. Damn near ruined the family jewels too," he added, unconsciously glancing at Harvey as he turned and entered the back room.

Nikalow caught the slip of the eye but didn't turn. Casually inspecting the fish displayed behind the glass cooler case, he moved to the end of the counter then turned to face the soft drink machine. Harvey was aware of the man but remained still, his hat hiding his face and a newspaper hiding his gun. Nikalow reached into his pocket and withdrew a hand full of change. As he picked through it a coin slipped from his hand and fell to the floor, coming to rest near Harvey's feet.

"Excuse me," Nikalow stated politely as he bent to retrieve the coin.

Harvey lifted his hat slightly, eyed the coin then with his foot, easily nudged it across the floor to Nikalow who paused and looked up into Harvey's face.

"Thank you," he stated flatly, picking up the coin.

Harvey offered no response as he stretched out his arms, locking his hands behind his head and adjusting his hat to its original position, his gun still available, resting comfortably in the classified section.

Escara reentered the room wheeling a hand truck stacked three crates high with iced fish. He chilled when he viewed the two men poised silently by the soda machine.

"Um… come on outside here, Mr. Nikalow, and I'll load this stuff up for ya," he suggested nervously.

Nikalow and Escara exited the market. Through the rusty screen door Harvey watched as the crates of fish were loaded in a white van parked at the end of the small lot. Escara returned for a second load and once that was delivered there was little verbal exchange as he accepted a large package, shoved it in an empty fish crate and stacked it on the hand truck with the other empties he had removed from the van. They shook hands and Nikalow drove off into the hot busy traffic nearby.

Chapter Eleven

A broad stripe ran the length of the executive jet's light blue fuselage extending to a sharp point on the wing. Where the stripe from each side of the aircraft met at the nose beneath the windshield they formed the wings of a raven in flight silhouetted against a pale moon. The aircraft whispered through soft white clouds as it lost altitude and burst into open sky. Below was the clear emerald ocean surrounding the island of Barbados. As the jet slid gracefully through the sky making it's landing approach, Captain Arthur Elliot eased back in the plush high-back seat and relished the view of a three-masted schooner with full sail, cutting easily through the water below.

Elliot was more relaxed now than he had been in days, finally solving the problem of the Dolphin Retriever presented to him by Whitemoon. Upon notification, Whitemoon had insisted Elliot take a vacation and visit him on his small island. He owned the island lock, stock and barrel and named it Heritage Place. Elliot accepted the invitation, taking fifteen days of overdue leave from the Navy. The idea of a vacation on the private tropical island of

Heritage Place in obviously very comfortable circumstances was appealing, if not irresistible.

When the jet was secured after landing the pilot moved through the craft to Elliot, "You'll transfer to a helicopter here, sir. There's no airstrip on the small island."

He escorted him off the aircraft where they immediately faced the helicopter with its long blades slowly slicing the air in anticipation of Elliot's boarding and lift off. Elliot boarded and seated himself, the jet pilot closed and secured the door from the outside and the helicopter heaved upward, leaned and headed out to sea.

The short flight to the island west of Barbados would be most interesting, thought Elliot. He enjoyed flying and with the helicopter maintaining a low altitude he could view the coral reefs and colorful sea bottom. Perhaps he would do some diving, he thought. It's been a while. Almost as long as the Dolphin project has lasted. Much too long.

Elliot was lost in thought as Whitemoon's private paradise rushed out of the horizon. It spread roughly through the water about twelve miles long by eight miles wide with small hills rising to the southern tip. It was covered with dense greenery and from the air a large inlet appeared to nearly split the island in two. As the helicopter approached, the surface water of the inlet vibrated from the down draft of the rotating blades. Hovering, then sliding to the hilly southern shore of the inlet, it came to rest on the roof of a large boathouse. He caught a brief glimpse of the classic Trumpy yacht Raven moored in the shelter of the house along with what appeared to be a sleek new 140 foot Hatteras sporting an exceptional amount of communications and satellite gear above decks.

The throbbing blades of the aircraft had slowed to a low-geared whoosh, when the door was opened. A tall muscular dark skinned man stood silent, staring and sizing up the newly arrived guest. He then grabbed Elliot's bags and turned away. Elliot leaped to the landing pad and immediately noticed the air was heavy and hot but smelled pleasantly of sea and flora. The man turned, offering a slight motion for him to follow as he walked across the pad to a stone stairway leading up a hill and then disappearing into a densely planted but well-groomed garden. Elliot followed to eventually emerge out of the garden and face a sprawling contemporary mansion also made of stone and featuring large tinted windows that gifted its residents with a complete view of the inlet and the ocean beyond.

Elliot paused, taking in the beauty of the island as it seemed to hold the mansion maternally in its arms. Below and across the inlet, smaller dwellings of similar design worked their way around the coast. Dark skinned people busied themselves near small boats and children played happily in the clear clean water. To Elliot, the entire place was postcard perfect.

"Welcome, Captain," Whitemoon greeted as he strolled from the house to the edge of the stone lined pool that complimented the natural flow of the landscape. "Please come in. Rest yourself."

Elliot was amazed, not only by the beautiful world Whitemoon had created but by his cordiality as well. "Thank you, sir," Elliot returned with a smile. "I had no idea it would be so beautiful here."

"Yes, it is that, Captain," Whitemoon smiled, taking in the island with pride. "My people have completed a near impossible task here."

"Your people?" questioned Elliot, surprised at Whitemoon's smile. He formerly thought the man was incapable of showing emotion.

"Yes, Captain, my people. Brought together after centuries of disruptive slavery, genocide and near extinction. You would know them as American Indians," Whitemoon turned to enter the mansion, "Come Captain."

Elliot could see it now, the crewman on the Raven, the pilots of the jet and helicopter and here on the island, all the people carried the proud lineage of a distant race and though

Whitemoon himself showed less than the others, it was evident in him as well.

"You've never expressed any curiosity regarding my name or lifestyle, Captain," Whitemoon continued as they seated themselves in the air-conditioned comfort of the great room. "Were you not curious in your dealings with me that I may have been perhaps some rich eccentric fool?"

Elliot was not sure how to answer, knowing rich and eccentric wasn't restricted to any certain race of people. "I had my reservations, I must admit," he said politely.

Whitemoon laughed "Let me put your mind at ease," he said as he accepted a cool glass of wine from a young girl who had been waiting when they entered. She offered the same to Elliot. "I am rich, Captain, in heritage as well as money. My people, or should I say ancestors, were a strong and proud nation, expanding from what is now New England into Canada. Needless to say, history speaks for itself. Due to the deceitful agreements of the invading Europeans and tribal wars, my people came to near extinction." Whitemoon stood, savoring his wine as he continued. "One so called Governor or Landlord of a part of the New England area we now call the State of Massachusetts, apparently suffered guilt of some sort. I suppose, compared to our contemporary society, there was a great deal of honor then though much of it was pretentious. Just the same, this gentleman took in a small tribe consisting of less than fifty weary Cayuga warriors and their families who had been driven from their homeland of central Pennsylvania by Europeans and fought their way north through enemy Algonquin tribes. They were warriors of the highest degree, proud brothers of the Mohawks, Oneida, Onondaga and Seneca. This Landlord appealed to their pride by trading them land for their protective services. As a result they assimilated, their children becoming educated to the white man's standards, many of them attending European schools to return and wed wealthy landowners.

One such… *fortunate* child was the daughter of the Cayuga chief known as *Whitemoon Raven.*"

As Whitemoon paused and reflectively gazed through the window to the inlet, Elliot rose and moved across the room to inspect a museum-like array of Indian relics lining the full length of the wall.

"I own much of that land to this day, Captain," Whitemoon stated proudly as he crossed the room to Elliot's side. "And no man will ever take it from me."

On the wall in the center of a display of Indian weapons hung a portrait of a young man wearing the uniform of the United States Army Special Forces.

"Who is this?" Elliot asked.

Whitemoon turned, ignoring the question. "Will you show our guest to his room," he directed the girl. "Our island is yours, Captain, for as long as you care to visit. After dinner we shall discuss your findings concerning the Dolphin and then I must be off early tomorrow morning. However anything you need will be provided so please do not hesitate to ask. Good afternoon." He turned and exited the mansion to be met at the pool by the same man who greeted Elliot on the landing pad.

Elliot stood silent, his eyes returning to the young man's portrait on the wall. "Who is he?" he asked the girl.

"He was Whitemoon's son," she answered.

"Was?"

"He was killed in Vietnam in 1968."

"Does he have any other family?"

"No," she answered flatly. "His wife died in a plane crash. Whitemoon is the sole survivor of his tribe. If you will follow me, sir." She picked up Elliot's bags and led him to his room.

That evening an elaborate dinner consisting of local cuisine was feasted on by Whitemoon, Elliot and two prominent Heritage residents. They discussed their task of converting the now beautiful and productive island from the once insect ridden wasteland of eight years prior. The technical barriers they had overcome fascinated Elliot. He unceasingly asked questions and supported their similar plans involving two other nearby uninhabited islands. At the conclusion of the dinner Whitemoon extended his apologies to his local guest and requested Elliot join him in his library. Once they were comfortably situated and away from the others Whitemoon inquired about Elliot's finding on the Dolphin's mishap.

"As you know, the Dolphin was designed to retrieve otherwise irretrievable equipment from the ocean floor." schooled Elliot. "Mainly strategic and research equipment dropped and self anchored at a sometimes precarious attitude on uneven terrain or extreme depths."

Whitemoon followed him with interest.

"The Dolphin is designed to adjust to any attitude required and then magnetically affixes itself to the object in question, whether it be seismographic measuring devices, military monitoring devices or, as in your case, a torpedo or missile. Homing in on a pre-designated signal received by the Dolphin and put out by your sub-container, the Dolphin, according to its programming, did exactly as it was supposed to do."

"By retrieving a man?" asked Whitemoon.

"No. By retrieving the surfboard," explained Elliot. "You see, the computer of the Dolphin, once it has reached its target, sends out a kind of sonar signal which reflects an image of the target object back to itself. Using this, the computer actually forms a picture of the target and maneuvers the Dolphin into position to retrieve it. I'm sure what happened is the Dolphin and the sub-container were operating in reasonably shallow water. The surfboard and surfer were apparently directly above the sub-container and the signal picked up by the Dolphin was a reflection of the board. The computer, functioning normally, pictured the board, adjusted the Dolphin accordingly and retrieved both board and man."

"But you said it has to fix itself magnetically to the object. Surfboards are plastic or fiberglass."

Elliot continued before Whitemoon could pose his question, "Exactly. That's what had me stumped so I broke off a piece of the board and check it out. The man was big and probably a good enough surfer not to be bothered by the slight extra weight of a custom made board with a metal flake finish. Covered, of course, with fiberglass. That puzzled me as well. The metal flake itself wouldn't constitute a decent magnetic pull however, once the Dolphin acquires the proper attitude around its target its eight long arm clamps close on it. The Dolphin itself then folds around the object and reverses in full thrust in order to free it from its anchor. The Dolphin then returns to the mother ship following a signal as before." Elliot sat back, pleased with his explanation.

"Then there is nothing to be corrected on the Dolphin?"

"Nothing. Just tell your people to keep an eye out for any surfers above the sub-container.

"I compliment you, Captain. And I apologize for the inconvenience of our last meeting. I sincerely hope that your vacation here will suffice to relieve any recent anxieties. That and the bonus you will find has been deposited in you bank account."

Whitemoon rose and extended his hand in gratitude. Elliot rose simultaneously and received his hand willingly.

"I understand you are a diving enthusiast."

"Yes," Elliot replied. "Though regretfully, I haven't had the opportunity for quite some time."

"My man Diongo is an excellent diver. I'll have him take you out tomorrow. I think you will find the waters in this area a fascinating diving experience."

They strolled through the mansion and out into the garden. The sun was setting with an array of deep soft rust orange colors as the blue grays of night hovered above. The inlet seemed to pause in anticipation of the coming darkness.

"I understand the reef at the north end of the island is quite colorful. Diongo has been there many times."

"Diongo? An Indian name?" asked Elliot.

"African actually," answered Whitemoon. "Diongo, like many of us, is the result of a diluted bloodline however in his case there are two direct and very strong lines, African and Mohawk. Some Mohawks were brought down to the Bahamas and sold into slavery. They were, of course, proud and uncontrollable, as was a certain group of African natives on the same island. Together they revolted and won their freedom but have remained in the islands. Those who choose to now reside here. Why don't you explore the inlet area, Captain? I think you will find the culture most interesting."

"I believe I will," accepted Elliot. "I can use the exercise."

As Elliot made his way down the hill to the inlet community, Diongo stepped out of the shadows beneath a large overhang of bougainvillea and came to Whitemoon's side.

"Da Columbia mun has arrived wit da merchandise," he informed Whitemoon.

"Excellent. Pay him and send him on his way then sort the cocaine and load the sub-container. I'll be leaving in the morning. I want you to stay here. Captain Elliot would like to do some diving on the north reef. I want you to accommodate him and make sure this dive is his last."

Diongo smiled, pivoted and walked off to the boathouse. Whitemoon stood and stared out over his island. His thoughts wondered from the colorful sunset to the silent white breakers of the beach far down in the distance. He felt alive and unified with the natural world that surrounded him, remembering the joy in planning and anticipation he and his son had shared. Whitemoon's face stiffened as he reminded himself of his new vow, his vow to destroy the society that vanquished his legacy and the government that killed his only boy.

The next morning Elliot felt better than he had in months as he strutted lightly down the stone path to the boathouse. Inhaling deeply, he took in the scent of tropical flowers and the pleasant sound of the many imported birds. At the base of the hill on the beach children darted in an out of the water. On a small dock adjoining the boathouse Diongo readied the gear for the day's diving venture to the north reef. A small girl squatted beside him carefully watching his every move as he checked the tanks and placed them in the sleek fiberglass outboard boat. He bent over the side and playfully splashed the girl lightly. She quickly dove off the dock and disappeared, surfacing on Diongo's blind side to douse him heavily in return. As he turned to catch her he spotted Elliot then turned back to the girl, said something in a language unrecognizable to Elliot and resumed his task. The girl looked up to Elliot then quickly swam off to join the other children.

"Mornin' Mista Elliot," said Diongo with a distinct Bahamian accent. "You ready for da wonders of da deep?"

"You bet. More than ready," smiled Elliot.

"Hop in, mun," said Diongo as he started the engine. "We got much water to travel."

Elliot cast off the mooring lines that secured the boat then boarded. Diongo eased the throttle forward, clearing the dock. They then cut through the inlet and out to sea, rounding the point to the north.

"It's a beautiful day, Diongo?" Elliot shouted over the noise of the motor.

"Yes Mista Elliot," agreed Diongo. "Always a beautiful day on dis island."

Elliot sat back soaking in the morning sun, his hair pushed back as the boat sped across the surface of the clear Caribbean ocean. Twenty minutes later Diongo eased back the throttle slightly and pointed. "Dare! You see?" Pointing to an area ahead of them. "Dare is da reef, Mista Elliot."

The boat slowed and Elliot began to assemble his gear.

"Now don't you get lost mun. Mista Whitemoon kick my black ass all da way back to St. George if you get banged up down dare."

"Aren't you coming down?"

"Yes sir," Diongo smiled. "I be down shortly. You go enjoy yourself. I gonna' take a look see da motor. I tink she runnin' a little loose."

Elliot rolled off the boat, splashing down into the silent world below. The sun streaked through the surface igniting the coral in an array of brilliant pastels. Fish darted to avoid the intruder then returned to curiously observe as he solemnly passed through their home to explore the sandy bottom. A second splash interrupted the surface and Elliot rolled over to see Diongo making his way through the water to join him. He continued along the bottom, rounding the reef, working deeper into a crevice of over-hanging coral. He turned again to see if Diongo had followed and saw air bubbles rising behind the protruding formation.

Elliot was moving lazily, enjoying the natural beauty of the reef and the abundant life it protected, poking occasionally at a shellfish on the sand when there came the sound of an engine. He turned and rose to rest on his knees on the bottom as he looked to the surface. The hull of Diongo's boat was moving slowly just above him. He then looked to the area where he had last seen him and saw bubbles were still rising. Confused, he looked again to the surface and saw two small objects splash into the water. Elliot was about to surface when the chilling recognition of the objects settled in his mind. Kicking furiously to find escape, he lunged backwards into a mass of coral, ripping the flesh across his shoulder. Realizing now there was no escape; he desperately backed into the sandy bottom extending his arms in a futile effort to protect himself. The grenades came closer, his eyes widened with fear and air bubbles surged from around his mouthpiece as he screamed into the now blood clouded water. The first grenade exploded, the force pounding him into the sand, ripping the mask from his face and tearing away his mouthpiece. Blood shot from his nose and ears as the second grenade, careened through the water by the blast of the first, bounced off the coral overhang and detonated mere inches from Elliot's face.

Above, Diongo pulled on his diving mask and was about to enter the water when he noticed the dorsal fin of a shark. He removed the mask, leaned over the side of the boat and set the mask on the surface of the water to act as a window. Below he saw another shark eagerly making for the coral crevasse where there emerged a large cloud of deep red blood. "Ah, be no cleanin' up here, Diongo," he laughed, then tossed the mask to the back of the boat, plopped into the seat and thrust the throttle forward for full power. The glistening bow rose in triumph as the boat plowed through the shining clear morning sea. "Yes Mista Elliot," Diongo laughed sadistically, "It's always a beautiful day on dis island."

Chapter Twelve

The phone rang several times before Harvey felt comfortable enough to answer. Even then he was hesitant. It had been four days since his encounter on the boat with Jack Escara. It had taken that long for him to realize what he had gotten into and the consequences of possible failure. He was committed now however and saw no way out other than successfully completing his extortion scheme and getting away quickly.

"Yeah," he answered carefully.

"Mr. Harvey, I believe you have been expecting my call?"

"That depends," Harvey tested. "What's on your mind?"

"Mr. Harvey, I haven't the time or the patience to play games. I know who you are. You have something that is mine and I want it."

"Yeah, well, it ain't yours no more. Let's call it a down payment." Harvey's confidence grew as he began to make his demands, "I got about six hundred thousand bucks here that just might buy my silence." He paused. "You listenin' there, buddy?"

"Yes, Mr. Harvey. I'm listening."

"Good. Then listen to this. I like round numbers. Say an even million. That would guarantee my silence for a long time. You understand me boy? That's a million cash on top of what I already got."

"Really, Mr. Harvey. You haven't the slightest idea who we are and you can't possibly believe you can get away with this."

Harvey grew uncontrollably angry, irritated at the calm exchange of the man on the phone and at his own foolish thoughtlessness. He was frightened, thinking now he should have taken the money and ran but he couldn't back down, not now. His greed and pride wouldn't let him. "Damn it, boy, you listen and listen good. I want a million bucks in cash put in a canvas bag and left on the floating dock at Fort Matanzas tonight. Midnight tonight. You got no choice. You understand? You pay up now or I'll hit every drop you make. And don't think I haven't covered my ass. You try and mess with me and I'll ruin your whole damn ball game."

"Mr. Harvey, you are either a fool or very resourceful, however as you say I may not have a choice. The money will be delivered as per your instructions and I expect you will then cease your demands. You understand that further such complications would be inconvenient for all concerned?"

"Is that what you call it, complications?" Harvey laughed nervously.

"Let's put it this way Mr. Harvey, time is not on your side."

"No, let's put it this way you arrogant sum'bitch, you just deliver the money and let me worry about my time." With that Harvey concluded the call.

At the other end of the line Whitemoon slowly replaced the telephone receiver. If he was angry or displeased it was not evident.

At 4:00 a.m. the next morning Harvey was cruising slowly south on Route A1A, confident he had carefully worked everything out. His boat was moored under the bridge that spanned the Matanzas where it met the ocean, placed there the day before. If they were following him now, thought Harvey, they would expect him to return to his car after picking up the money. He would grab it then run up river to a small cove where he had another car parked and waiting. He knew the river well, certainly better than whoever he was up against. They were playing his game now, he thought, on his turf by his rules.

The morning sun, still below the horizon strained a dim gray into the sky as Harvey slowly drove across the bridge. To be sure he wasn't followed he continued past Summer Island to Marineland then turned around and drove back to the bridge with his car lights off. Upon arrival he parked at the south end of the bridge, removed an assault rifle from the trunk, then scurried down into the dark shadows below where he had stowed the boat.

Unleashing the boat, he pushed it easily into the shadows beneath the bridge where he sat silent, waiting for enough light to allow him a clear view of the old small Spanish outpost and its dock. The sun struggled and forced its way slowly from the depths of the Atlantic sending the first dim early morning light across the Matanzas. The isolated old Spanish landmark, resting peacefully on an outcropping of Rattle Snake Island, defined itself in a gray green haze. Harvey focused his binoculars on the dock below. The money was there.

A nervous smile spread over his face as he mounted the rifle within easy reach and started the engine. The sound of the muffled inboard echoed under the bridge as the boat moved slowly from the shadows and along the dark side of the river. When he was less that a hundred yards from the dock and satisfied that all was safe, he shoved the throttle forward, lifting the boat radically as it surged through the water. He would have to get the bag on the first pass, he thought, if anyone was there he couldn't give them time to get off an accurate shot. *His* river, he thought. Nobody could beat him on his river.

Harvey approached the dock at full speed, pulled back on the throttle and quickly turned the boat, ramming its hull full length against the side. He grabbed wildly for the canvas bag, nearly dropping it in the water as the boat rocked and came away from the dock. Tossing the heavy sack on the seat next to him he jammed the throttle forward, secured the rifle in a firing position above the windshield with one hand and steered the boat with the other. His stomach churned in anticipation as he made his way over the dark water. Looking over his shoulder he was amazed that no one had appeared from behind or atop the fort. It was too easy, he thought, or maybe he just outsmarted them.

The river curved north and became darker as it wound behind the big island. After a few minutes he slowed and relaxed then reached over and began opening the bag. At that moment a blinding spotlight hit him straight on and automatic weapons fire ripped across the windshield missing him but blasting open the sack sending small sheets of newspaper flying into the air like large confetti. Harvey fell to the deck, quickly grabbing his rifle but remaining there as though he were dead, his unguided boat circling aimlessly. Over the sound of his idling engine he could hear another. It was approaching slowly, the spotlight still bright and holding steady. He crawled forward within reach of the wheel and throttle and waited.

When the approaching craft was closer he cut the throttle, stood and blasted away, knocking out the light and the man with the weapon. He then rammed the throttle forward and raced back toward the bridge. He heard the boat behind him gain power and turned and fired again but missed. He was answered by the relentless spray of an automatic weapon that ripped open his shoulder and literally blew off his right ear, knocking him forward into a blood splattered shattered windshield. Rounding the curve of the river, he viewed an amazing blood red and yellow sunrise silhouetting the bridge as it rushed toward him. I'm going to make it, he thought. My river and I'm going to make it.

Once again bullets ripped the transom of his boat, this time killing the engine. Harvey had lost the race. In a desperate effort, he turned and aimed at his oncoming doom but before he could squeeze the trigger a heavy WHOMPH forced him back into the wheel. The intense heat of the explosion of the other boat seared his face as he stared in shock at his pursuers fiery death. Debris from their boat rained down and sizzled into the water around him, then the Matanzas grew deathly silent.

Harvey searched in all directions for another boat, wondering who had so effectively come to his rescue. His search eventually settled on the top of the bridge as he floundered helplessly, his torn shoulder oozing blood over the scattered worthless newspaper money and dripping over the side into the river. He sat there helpless, bobbing on the surface of the Matanzas. Matanzas, Spanish for *the river of blood*. As he looked up to the bridge he thought it ironic to be sitting there at the very spot where the river had earned its name. Where four centuries earlier the deceitful Spanish had persuaded a ship full of weary storm torn stranded Frenchmen to surrender so they could receive aid and comfort. Surrendering a handful at a time they were systematically taken out of view and hacked to pieces, butchered to the extent that their blood turned the river red becoming the Matanzas. The same Matanzas now turning red with the blood of another fool, thought Harvey.

On the bridge a lone figure stood poised in front of a rising deep yellow sun. Harvey stared, weak, puzzled. He fell back into the seat. Nikalow slowly reloaded the M-79 grenade launcher, aimed it expertly at Harvey, smiled and fired.

Chapter Thirteen

"**I**'ll bet you're a real ladies man," Carol smiled as she filled Chris' glass with more iced tea. The young boy glowed with silent embarrassment and looked to his father who was tending the steaks on the grill. His father simply smiled as he tossed some of his beer on the flaming charcoals to cool them and avoid burning the meat.

"I'm not sure if it's a blessing or a curse at his age," Majors stated then turned to Ramsey to continue their conversation. "I couldn't believe it when you called, Ram. Of all people. And still in the Navy."

"Still in the Navy," Ramsey echoed. "And I still eat my steaks rare."

"I honestly didn't think you would stay in. Not after what I saw you go through in Nam."

"Insecurity I guess," Ramsey answered. "Or indecision. What the hell else can I do?"

"Politics," stated Majors. "What happened to that college degree and all that honor and justice for all stuff?"

"Ask Nixon," laughed Ramsey. "Hell, Frank, I think I'd rather be back in Vietnam than try and make it in that snake pit." He reached into a cooler and withdrew two fresh beers, tossing one to the grill master. "And what about you?" he continued. "I thought you were going to be the next Edward R. Murrow."

"Oh hell, I thought I was."

Both men laughed as they sampled the beer.

"Guess the freckles didn't get along with the camera, huh Frank? Color TV and all that."

"I think freckles are cute," Carol defended. "I've got a few myself, you know."

"Yes, I know," smiled Ramsey.

"You ass," retorted Carol.

Majors stared down into the white-hot coals as he passed through his mind the many reasons he had used to discontinue his profession. They all seemingly came to one end, his wife. He suffered when she died, not only because of her death but greatly due to the guilt from all the times he left her alone and skipped off around the world as a journalist reporting on distant wars and other peoples' misery, not thinking of the lonely misery she must have felt in his absence. She never complained and he foolishly plunged forward, building his career but leaving her to reach out with letters written through tears as she savored quick glimpses of him, courtesy of the nightly network news.

"You're a damn good journalist, Frank. Why give it up?" asked Ramsey.

Majors looked across the grill at Chris who was secretly admiring Carol as she set the table. "Let's just say I couldn't take it anymore, old buddy. You know, no news is good news and whatever bad news there is… well, as our friend Nixon would say, they won't have Frank Majors to push around anymore."

"I understand," Ramsey acknowledged and both men knew that each understood too well.

"Hey listen you guys," said Carol. "How come I haven't heard any great war stories yet? A couple of bona fide heroes like you should be able to tell some real doozies. Right Chris?"

"Yeah, Dad! Tell the one about the applesauce."

Ramsey immediately began to laugh, "Damn Frank, do you really tell that story?"

"Only on cold snowy nights. Besides, it's hardly a secret, buddy. I'm surprised it never made the evening news," Majors stated as his face flushed.

"Okay heroes, what's the big mystery?" Carol demanded.

"You tell her, Ram. Hell, it was your idea in the first place," said Majors.

"Are you kidding? I've never told that story!"

"Confession time old buddy," said Majors as he turned the steaks.

"Yeah, fess up hero," demanded Carol. "Or I'll cut you off for a week."

Chris laughed and Carol quickly realized what she had said.

"My God!" she blurted in surprise of Chris' quick perception.

"Believe it, Carol," Majors laughed. "These kids don't miss a trick now days."

"Okay, okay," Ramsey conceded. "But you have to keep in mind that we were sto... I mean drunk at the time."

"You were stoned out of your gourd," corrected young Chris.

Majors cleared his throat in the boy's direction who doused his words with some iced tea.

"Anyway," Ramsey continued. "We both weaseled a few days off from the war and went chopper hopping until we got to Saigon where we commenced to do a little enthusiastic partying until these MPs picked us up because there was a curfew. They didn't lock us up but did restrict us to their compound for the night. Well, we were pi... um, ticked off of course because we only had that one night so we spent a good deal of it plotting revenge."

"Tell her about the applesauce," insisted Chris.

"Hang in there kid. It's coming," Ramsey replied.

"Yeah, tell me about the applesauce," echoed Carol.

Ramsey leaned forward in his lounge chair to add a little drama to his story. Carol leaned forward holding Chris' hand in anticipation.

"So, there we were, mad as hell at the MPs," he continued angrily. "So we painted up our faces with camouflage and crept through the compound to the mess hall. We snuck into…"

"Sneaked," corrected Carol.

"What?"

"Never mind," she said. "Go on, go on."

"Okay… into the mess hall and jumped the night baker, tied him up and got into the food storage. At first we just wanted to pig out and escape but we found these three cases of dehydrated applesauce and some powdered red fruit drink mix. So we decided to… well, we went out and climbed the water tower and dumped it all in."

"In? You mean, in the water in the tower?" asked Carol.

Ramsey nodded a yes and Chris began to laugh uncontrollably.

"And dad fell in! He fell into the water!"

"You bet he did," continued Ramsey. "He swam around and mixed that junk up so well and it got so thick he could hardly get out. I had to get a rope and pull him out and when I saw him… oh, hell, talk about the original bloody Mary!"

Chris and Carol were rolling with laughter, Chris spilling his drink on Carol's slacks.

"And this S.O.B. started laughing so hard," Majors broke in, pointing the spatula at Ramsey, "He woke up the entire damn compound. We damn near got our asses blown off!"

"Yeah, but… but you should have seen those bastards when they got in the showers the next morning!" Ramsey rolled with laughter. "Red gunk…red MPs… everywhere! It was like that movie, The Blob!"

"Did they catch you? What did they do to you?" asked Carol.

"Well, Ram tried to tell them it was a Viet Cong sapper and we were trying to capture him but that didn't hold up to well considering I was coated in red applesauce. So we finally just confessed," stated Majors. "I mean, what could they do, send us to Vietnam?"

"I think they were too embarrassed to really do us any serious damage," added Ramsey. "They put us on a chopper the next day and sent us off."

"Not exactly," corrected Majors. "Would you believe they sent a formal complaint to the network and I got stuck with a bill?"

Ramsey stood and faced Majors, "Oh, hey buddy, I'm really sorry about that. I didn't know," he lied.

"Bull shit," Majors replied, grinning at Ramsey.

"Yeah, but wasn't it worth it?" asked Ramsey. "Besides, you were overpaid anyway."

"Every penny," Majors agreed. "Every single penny."

"Eight hundred and sixty-three bucks," injected Chris.

"And forty-eight cents," laughed Majors. "I still have the receipt."

Carol laughed easily as she watched Ramsey happily engulfed in the past. She had just seen a part of him that was rare and delightful. Missing was the usual preoccupation which nagged their relationship. She liked what she saw. She would keep him, she thought, no matter what the cost.

"Steaks are up," announced Majors. "Chris, go get your brother and then get the baked potatoes out of the oven."

"I'll help you, lover boy," said Carol as she rose and followed the boy inside the house.

"Seems like a million years ago, doesn't it?" said Ramsey.

"Yeah. A million years and still just yesterday. Time is funny that way.

"Nice kids," Ramsey stated, sitting and leaning back in the lounge chair.

"Nice girl," returned Majors.

"Yeah," Ramsey agreed with a smile.

Both men were lost in silent memories as Majors placed the steaks carefully on their plates. Ramsey then broke the silence when he inquired about the welfare of his friend's oldest son, Tony.

"He'll be okay," Majors stated. "He's a strong kid. Like his mother."

"I read about it in the paper. They never recovered the body?"

"No. I doubt if they will. It's a big ocean. Strange though. About the board, I mean. They recovered a piece of it. They should have found all of it. It's like he was swallowed up by a damn whale or something."

Majors seemed to grow angry at the thought. Ramsey had seen the look before, in Vietnam when things got bad and he could do nothing to change it. It was a frustration born of confusion and wonder. They had all felt it in their own way. Frank Majors' because he was supposed to be on the outside looking in, to be an objective observer and reporter.

"So, you haven't told me why you're here, old buddy. Did the Navy send you down to check for applesauce in the Matanzas Bay?"

"No," laughed Ramsey. "More like poking in the dark, actually. I've got a corpse and a lot of unanswered questions."

"'Nuff said, my man. My grill is bugged and we don't want to jeopardize the security of this great nation," laughed Majors.

"Hey Dad!" Chris called from the house. "Steve is on the phone and Carol burnt her finger!"

"I'll get the phone and leave the medical aid to the Navy," said Majors as both men entered the house.

"Steve and his wife were supposed to be here for dinner weren't they?" asked Ramsey.

"Yeah. Steve's a cop. He's probably calling to apologize. Works lousy hours and all that."

Ramsey patronized Carol's burnt thumb as Majors spoke on the kitchen phone.

"It's okay. No problem. We'll just have to force ourselves to eat a couple of extra steaks," Majors spoke into the phone. "What's the big event anyway?"

The kitchen group was silent as Majors listened to Steve's description of events that took place on the Matanzas early that morning.

"Two boats? Who got killed? Harvey. That's the guy on the beach. The Marine Patrolman." He listened to Steve a few more moments then concluded the conversation. "No problem, Steve. No apologies necessary. We'll do it again soon." He replaced the receiver and they returned to the patio.

"Can't make it?" asked Ramsey as he made his way through the door with a plate full of baked potatoes.

"No. Seems two boats blew up down river. Steve was supposed to get off this morning but he's got to work straight through and help sort things out. Some folks heard machine gun fire before the explosions."

"Sounds like drug smugglers," suggested Ramsey.

"Yeah, probably. Killed a marine patrolman named Harvey. I met him the other day on the beach when Blacky disappeared. They found two dead floaters. Harvey died in the hospital. Steve is trying to make sense of it all."

The boys and Carol came out of the house wheeling steak sauce and other condiments as Majors continued.

"Not much to go on I guess. Steve said Harvey mumbled something about paper and some guy named Nikalow. I guess they've got their hands full with..."

"What?" interrupted Ramsey.

"Said they... I mean,- Steve's got his hands full with this stuff and summer has just started..."

"No, no. You said this guy said something before he died," Ramsey said, his interest peaking. Not sure of what he heard.

"Oh yeah, he said something about paper and... um, Nikalow. Why?"

"Oh... nothing," came Ramsey, picking up his beer and taking a long thoughtful gulp. "Thought you said something else."

"Carol, what do you say we pick up our things and check into a motel here in town," said Ramsey as though he were suddenly inspired.

"No need," Carol returned quickly as she chewed a tasty cut of steak.

"What?" questioned Ramsey.

"No need to. I packed everything this morning and put it in the trunk.

"You did what?"

"Yep, I did. Didn't really like that Turtle place anyway. Hey lover, hand me the ketchup," she said, turning to Chris.

Chris passed her the ketchup and smiled at Ramsey. He then turned and whispered something to Tony and they both giggled.

"Does anyone want to let me in on what's going on?" Ramsey asked.

"She called a motel when she was in the kitchen," laughed Chris.

"Yeah, so what?" Ramsey challenged Chris.

"She told them the room was for two nuns," the boy explained as he burst into laughter.

"Yeah, well... sometimes she has a little problem with reality," answered Ramsey. "Like when she chops up kids and turns them into dog food."

Chris stared at Ramsey for a long serious moment then stated through a mouth full of food, "Bull shit."

Chapter Fourteen

"Captain Downs, this is Commander Lightner."

"Yes Commander, what can I do for you?"

Ramsey adjusted the phone on his shoulder and flipped through his notebook. "Sir, I'm in St. Augustine and I'm picking up on a few things here. I may need some assistance. Also, I've been expecting some information from Admiral Peters. Has it arrived? It would have been sent to my attention through your office."

"I haven't received anything yet, Commander. I'll forward an inquiry. Give me the information on the request."

"I need any and all information on an individual, system or operation known as *Whitemoon*. The same on an individual known as *Nikalow* and a background on a Theresa Coggin of Denver, Colorado. Also an extended file search on our stiff, Dillair. Priority check, interagency."

Downs made a few notes and passed them on to his clerk. "Hold on Commander," he said as he motioned for his clerk to take instruction. "Judy, get me Captain Hughes at the Pentagon." He then continued his conversation with Ramsey,

"Listen Commander, I think I can expedite that info for you, no problem. Now, what kind of assistance do you need?"

"Can you spare Lieutenant Eisen?"

"No problem. Where and when?"

"Sir, you're too easy."

"Not at all, Commander," Downs smiled into the phone. "I'm a short timer, remember? And I'm more than willing to let you young'ns carry the load, if you know what I mean."

"I think I do, sir." Ramsey could feel the Captain's cordiality through the phone. He imagined it was that very thing which ended a long career at the rank of Captain and not Admiral. The man probably had all the qualities and talent necessary for higher rank except the ability or willingness to be a complete jerk. "If you could, will you have Eisen meet me at my motel. Tell him to hand carry whatever info comes down the pike on my request. Also tell him to wear civvies. By the way, what is the crime situation in St. Augustine?"

"Not much to speak of. Down right dull actually. I hear you can even walk the streets at night."

"Thank you Captain. I'll keep you informed."

"It's your show, Commander. You just yell when you need help."

As Ramsey discontinued the telephone conversation with Captain Downs, Carol returned from the motel pool still dripping and smelling of suntan lotion.

"How about dinner and a show?" proposed Ramsey.

"Dinner sounds great but I can take in a movie any time. How 'bout dinner and sex?" suggested Carol as she started for the shower.

"No, I mean a show. You know, music, dancers... Indians."

"Indians?"

"Right."

"Sounds like *Annie Get Your Gun*. God spare me, Ramsey. I really can't abide amateur theater," she pleaded over the sound of the shower.

"Naked Indians."

"What?"

"Big, tall, dark, naked Indians," Ramsey announced as he slid open the shower door and held up a brochure of pictures from *The Cross and The Sword* production at the St. Augustine Amphitheater. The Indians weren't actually nude but who could tell in the fog of a shower, thought Ramsey. He was more interested in the performance of one dancer than the full show. He needed to speak again with Dillair's girl, Theresa Coggin. He tried earlier that day but the girl wasn't home. At the show he could catch her back stage and ask a few very important questions. He needed to know how Dillair earned his bread and butter and what happened to the letter he wrote the last night he was with her. Nikalow was becoming a real character as well and she was Ramsey's only link. He felt he had to act fast. Aside from people getting killed, there was something else that gave him a sense of urgency. A feeling of something bizarre and if there was one thing constant in Ramsey's life it was his trust in his own instincts which never seemed to fail him.

Upon the recommendation of Frank Majors, Ramsey and Carol dined at a local restaurant on the island. Ramsey wanted shrimp but Carol insisted on oysters, for purely selfish reasons of course. They compromised and had both. From there they went to the amphitheater to take in the history of the settlement of St. Augustine by way of symphonic drama. As the play unfurled, Theresa Coggin made her entrance as the Indian Princes Notina. She was a pivotal character and the center of attraction in a fertility dance that Ramsey took to be fairly appealing and he discovered she wasn't merely a dancer but an actress as well, a good one, causing him to wonder why she was wasting her efforts here. He had seen her up close, stoned and miserable, she was still beautiful. He was sure she could make it big in New York or Hollywood.

During the intermission he excused himself to Carol under the pretense of going to the restroom. Instead, he went back stage to arrange a meeting after the performance. He found her sitting quietly near the dressing room, staring aimlessly. Nearby, a male Indian was making out with a Spanish dancer and a few Spanish soldiers were discussing the problem of the cannon not firing in the battle scene the night before.

Miss Coggin," he said as he approached slowly. "Miss Coggin, I'm Commander Lightner. I spoke to you the other day about Fred Dillair."

She gazed at him without recognition.

He continued, "I need to speak with you again. Perhaps after the show?"

She sat silent.

"About the letter Fred wrote the last night you saw him."

"I have it," she said softly. "I read it. My god, I read it!" She stood, searching Ramsey's eyes for understanding. She began to reach out to him when she suddenly froze. Her eyes widened as they settled on a shadowed figure poised near a stage entrance. Ramsey turned. Through a group of dancers who were rehearsing an upcoming scene he caught a quick glimpse of a man as he moved into the shadows toward the seating area of the theater. Ramsey turned back to Theresa.

"Miss Coggin, I need to speak with you after the show." As he spoke, the theater lights dimmed and a speaker in the dressing room announced the last call for the second act.

"My name is Dillair. Theresa Dillair."

Ramsey stared in surprise. The players moved toward the stage area and she was pulled away, moving clumsily as she glared back at Ramsey. In her eyes Ramsey didn't see grief for a lost husband but despair.

The second act opened with a dim spotlight on a quartet of Spanish settlers as they sent a melancholy tune through the dense air of the theater. Ramsey returned to his seat.

"What took you so long? Thought you flushed yourself to China. And you didn't even bring me some popcorn," stated Carol while focusing on the stage. "Humph, some date. Didn't even bring pop corn."

In spite of her emotional state Theresa performed well throughout the second act in which a theatrical hurricane brought famine to the young colony and lead to an all out battle between the settlers and the Indians. Pedro Menendez de Avilles, the Spanish Governor, and the Indian Princess Notina faced a poetic, if not Shakespearian, love tragedy with the death of one or both being the inevitable solution. In this case it was the Princess Notina, Theresa Coggin Dillair, rushing to her lover in the midst of battle. Amid canon fire, screams of agony, and clashing swords and spears, she is fallen by the killing instrument meant for her Spanish lover. After this tragic turn of fate the battle ends and women cry as death lingers everywhere. Governor Menendez laments over the body of his beloved Indian Princes Notina, the play ends and the full company rises in song except for the celebrated Notina who lies still in Pedro's arms. Ramsey is quick to notice however that Pedro is obviously laboring nervously through the finale as he continues to hold and watch the princess. All lights fade to black. When the lights return the full company is standing, bowing, a girl screams. Ramsey sits up abruptly when he sees Theresa is still lying on the stage. The applause continues from the audience though most of them are ignorant of the reality of what they're seeing. Pedro is now kneeling near her, growing sick and finally regurgitating as the lights reveal the blood on his hands and blouse and the once beautiful Indian princess, Theresa Coggin Dillair, dead, her skull destroyed by a silent bullet.

While the audience views the confusion on stage, Ramsey quickly searches the perimeter of the amphitheater. The man who an hour before frightened Theresa, was now making his way calmly through the excited theater patrons toward the exit. Ramsey wedged his way through the crowd to the center isle, his eyes fixed on the tall man with the goatee. When the fleeing assassin reached the exit he paused then turned to look down on the mass of excitement he was leaving behind, evidently enjoying the entire scene.

The theater staff rushed down the center isle, nearly knocking Ramsey into the lap of a foreign tourist who looked at him with disgust, "A ridiculous American hoax," stated the irritated woman.

Ramsey quickly regained his stand, rushed to and through the exit, down the long garden walkway and into the dark parking lot finding no one. The killer had apparently fled with ease.

Hours later the police allowed the more than nine hundred witnesses to leave the theater, none of whom reported seeing anything other than an average Spanish-Indian war. Now Ramsey and Carol sat parked near Theresa's apartment on Cordova Street. Ramsey had fully expected to find the police waiting when they arrived but there were none. "I want you to sit here. Don't leave the car. If the police show up I want you to drive off but honk the horn as you go."

"What the hell's going on? What kind of damn spy are you? What the..."

"Will you shut up? I'm not a spy," Ramsey declared as he exited the car.

"What the hell is happening here, Ramsey? I mean people are dying," Carol was angry, more from the frustration of being uninformed or ignorant to the events taking place around her than the fact Ramsey and possibly even she was involved.

"People die all the time, Carol."

"Oh sure, with their brains on public display. If I'm going to suffer through an external lobotomy I would really like a little heads up first. No pun intended."

"Will you just shut up and do what I tell you. I'll explain later." Leaving it at that, Ramsey walked down the street, into the apartment house and slowly up the stairs. He froze near the top of the stairs when he came face to face with the old landlady's dog. Behind the dog he could see a dim light through the crack at the bottom of the door to Theresa's apartment. He took another step. The dog did the same but remained silent. Ramsey took another then another. The dog came closer with each step. When he reached the top of the dark stairs he paused, tense with the thought the dog would attack or begin to bark. Suddenly the dog darted for his leg. Ramsey's heart accelerated. Before he could react, he found the dog on its hind legs, the nails of its forepaws digging into his thigh as its nose shot into his crotch and began to sniff. Ramsey shoved the dog off and backed away, almost falling down the stairs. Grabbing the banister with his right hand, he pushed the dog aside with the other. The dog turned to him, blinked disappointment then slowly moved to the door of the neighboring apartment, sniffed, raised its leg and pissed on the welcome mat.

"Shit," sighed Ramsey as he carefully slid to the door at the end of the dark hall. He listened, holding his breath, thinking someone might be inside. There were no sounds other than the toenails of the dog on the hardwood floor as it followed Ramsey's progress. He tried the door and found it unlocked. Pushing it open slowly, he backed against the wall. Light filled the once dark hall apparently comforting the dog who settled on the doormat. Ramsey stepped over the creature and into the apartment he had visited the day before. This visit however revealed not the tidy and comfortable chamber of a beautiful woman but a savagely invaded disheveled dwelling of a frightened widow, Dillair's widow, and now, like her husband, she was dead.

The apartment had been searched thoroughly without respect or method, simply destroyed with efficient contempt. Maybe it was the man at the theater. Maybe he's Nikalow, thought Ramsey. He decided there was no reason to search further. If the letter had been there it surely had been found by whoever had beaten him to the apartment. He departed the place quickly and silently, the dog following him as far as the front door at the bottom of the stairs then returning to the top of the stairs where it sat waiting for its next victim.

As Ramsey walked down the street he could see Carol sitting in the car, angrily smoking a cigarette. He would have to tell her something, he thought. She wouldn't let up until he did. Perhaps he could stall her until they reached the motel then distract her with her favorite pastime, anything to allow her to cool off and give him time to think and regroup. He knew what it would take and suddenly he was glad they had oysters for dinner.

Chapter Fifteen

There was little or no breeze to relieve Cannon of the humidity typical to Washington, D.C. this time of year. He slowed his pace, removed his sports jacket and loosened his tie to get as comfortable as possible. His report today would not be easy to deliver. This, plus the usual discomfort of dealing with the Committee would prove to be most demanding.

As he walked through the park he half-heartedly viewed a polo match a hundred yards away and nearby was a group of black people engrossed in a down-home barbecue, all in the shadow of the Lincoln Memorial and all seemingly alien to its presence. Snobby highbrow horsemen, barbeque ribs, society want-to-be socialites, rap music, fried chicken and fat old ladies. Polo and soul, all on the same green. What a contrast and only in D.C., he thought. Cannon liked to think of Washington as a multi-tiered cake. In the sixties he once referred to it as a chocolate cake covered with white Anglo icing and decorated with multicolored international leeches. Each upper tier gets smaller, sweeter and richer. On top of the cake rest the non-perishable symbols of freedom, justice and equality, admired by all but never ever do they rest on the bottom layer.

Cannon missed the excitement and challenge of the sixties when he and the movement were active. Black men challenged the system and sent a chill through the social spine of an entire nation. Many of the leaders of the movement, men like himself, faded as did their cause, abandoned, claimed Cannon, left behind by the more successful. Those who found secure havens on a higher political or social level and forgot how they had arrived there and others who simply cashed in, making fortunes on their notoriety and ability to manipulate black public opinion or the black marketplace, becoming no better than those who had oppressed them for hundreds of years. Cannon felt they sold out. They however claimed wisdom by using the system to gain eventual change and acceptance. They were too few, he argued, and their way was too slow, selfish and compromising. Cannon was not a radical or extremist but then he was not a patient man. He would not rule out revolution, yet still feared the cost of such drastic action. He often found himself near insanity as he tried to reason his purpose and actions. He had given up trying to persuade his people, trying to educate them as to where they were and where they should be. He felt he had become a lingering echo falling on deaf ears. Ears too satisfied, too content with free lunches and mediocrity.

Now he worked for the Committee. He was their tool. They used him and he let them. They paid him well but he was no fool and knew should they succeed his money would mean nothing. If indeed they should succeed he doubted whether life would have any value at all. He had given up trying to understand them or anyone else for that matter. They already had power and wealth. They controlled much of the international markets, everything from peaches to petroleum, not to mention entire governments, regions, and monarchies. They were productive and intelligent. Indeed, what challenge would be left for them? Perhaps they felt some collective urge to create a corporate Shangri-La, some god-like motivation. What greater challenge exists then to create a single society from a world of conflicting nations and cultures? Cultures that have for thousands of years lived, prospered and died at each others expense in numbers and ways too horrible to remember yet too horrible to forget.

Cannon saw the future differently. A single world society, yes, it was inevitable with time. Years, hundreds of years, maybe thousands. It is their methods he questioned. They will encourage mass destruction, get someone else to push the button then step in as aftermath heroes and rebuild, reline, and reform the entire human race. Just the concept is so massive, so complex that it gave Cannon a headache to dwell on. He wanted to discuss alternatives but turned himself off at each opportunity. After all, who was he but a simple mechanism in a very large machine. The destruction will come anyway, they would say. In a year, in ten or thirty years. The human race is exactly that, only human. It has set its course for total elimination. Massive destruction is convenient they would say. It leaves less people to regulate and eliminates the urban problem areas and weaker masses. It will cancel out any lingering affection for the past and open the door for a beautiful new society. This is where Cannon disagreed. People are people, he thought. Some will always ride a high horse and inevitable social differences will emerge. A class separation will crawl through their perfect society and what goes around comes around and the whole damn mess goes down again. So why am I even here Cannon asked himself. Who even gives a damn? Maybe some giant egghead has got this whole fucking universe in a test tube and he's going to flush it down the shitter. Just do your job, Cannon tells himself as he has on other days, and let the rest of the world worry about the rest of the world.

He paused at the curb and lit a cigarette as a tourist filled bus rolled by. The smell of its diesel fumes flashed him back to his street days in Detroit. After crossing the street to another area of the park he lingered under a tree long enough to pick his contact out of the small crowd of parents and others who were observing two first year youth soccer teams perform a comedy of errors. The young players were confused and winded. The crowd was delighted. Cannon carefully and inconspicuously made his way to the side of the gentleman he had met before in the museum. And as before, the elderly gentleman opened the conversation.

"They call them Buzzers," Mr. Cannon.

"Buzzers?"

"Yes," the gentleman explained. "You see, they are new to the game and haven't quite got the grasp of their responsibilities. Yet they are so enthusiastic they blindly buzz about the ball in hopes of successfully completing a goal. Much like our world situation. Don't you agree?"

Cannon observed the game silently. Trying to bring together in his mind a tactful and subtle disclosure of recent events in St. Augustine.

The man continued, "What they need, Mr. Cannon, is a foundation, knowledge and execution. A stable overseer to insure and maintain continuity." The man turned away from the game and strolled slowly toward a line of large old trees bordering the field. Cannon followed. When they were clear of the crowd the man continued.

"Do you know why I sent for you?"

"Yes," replied Cannon.

"It is not necessary for you to relate what has happened. I am aware of everything." He paused to observe a squirrel rooting through the grass.

Cannon was surprised. He didn't know his Committee contact was so informed. It irritated him to entertain the thought that all of their previous meetings must have simply been entertaining tests of loyalty or security by the old man. Cannon felt foolish, thinking he should have suspected as much long ago.

"I'm interested in your evaluation of the situation, Mr. Cannon. And of course, a possible solution."

Cannon took a slow deep breath to insure a confident delivery, "To have gone this far without complication is, I feel, fortunate," he told the older gentleman. "I expected problems such as this long ago. The original breakdown was in Whitemoon's operation. We had to stand back because he is not aware of us. It was the missile technician and we took care of that situation but the Russian has acted too strongly. He's become a control problem. I can deal with that immediately. As for the series of deaths, I'm not really concerned. The authorities won't have time to put enough information together to prevent Whitemoon's success."

"I'm afraid I have to disagree, Mr. Cannon. It seems there is a Navy investigation in progress due to the death of the missile technician. It's being conducted by only one officer at this time. I can control the Washington end of whatever he may disclose, however I understand he is a very capable man. We need to deal with him"

Cannon was growing depressed with the idea of having to initiate the deaths of so many people yet he questioned his reaction. After all, he thought, he was a part of an overall plan of mass human elimination, genocide on a scale never before attempted. He flashed in his mind a picture of himself dressed as one of Hitler's finest. A black Nazi. The thought was comical. "I don't think another death would be wise just now. I think we can contain him."

"Very good, Mr. Cannon. I will depend on that. You will find a packet of information concerning this officer and the current extent of his knowledge of these affairs in your room when you return to your hotel. Be sure and deal with this Russian fellow however. I believe his name is Nikalow?"

"Yes," Cannon confirmed.

"If all goes well, I shouldn't see you again until after..." The gentleman paused. "Until we initiate phase one of the reconstruction. You will get to your safe haven in time, I assume?"

Cannon hesitated. He couldn't say what he truly felt. That it didn't matter. That he really didn't give a shit.

Chapter Sixteen

A large radio blared country music through an otherwise tranquil sunrise as the trawler Happy Jack plowed heavily due north off the coast of Ponte Vedra Beach. At the helm Jack Escara toyed with the bandage across his nose between sips of his morning coffee. He stood behind the wheel of the modified trawler and looked out to the bow where his young crewman sprawled lazily, nursing a cup of the same coffee and sucked a marijuana joint.

"Check it out below!" Jack ordered from the bridge. "She's comin' in!"

The young crewman raised himself slowly, searching through the surface of the water and upon sighting the incoming Dolphin Retriever, turned and started below.

Escara cut the engines to an idol. "Give a yell when she's in."

He sat back and drew a pack of cigarettes from his shirt pocket, smiling with the satisfaction of another problem free pickup, his last according to his deal with Whitemoon. The boat is now his, including the Dolphin. His only dilemma now was to decide how to use it. He had considered continuing drug pickups but that involved bringing in strange people he knew he couldn't trust. He had put away a lot of money and so he wasn't rushed to do anything at all but he was uncomfortable carrying around the dolphin after the incident with his old buddy, Stony. His best bet, he thought, would be to sell the Desco trawler and Dolphin down state. Someone would buy it, someone who could invest in another boat to make the drops. Yeah, thought Escara, it was time to get out while the getting was easy.

Below, the Happy Jack opened her hull and lowered a steel mesh net to embrace the Dolphin as it glided in beneath the boat. The boy cut its power by remote control, checked that it was nestled safely and then raised the net and the Dolphin holding Whitemoon's torpedo container. When it cleared the water he locked on four hooks cabled to winches that raised it above the net. The net then rolled back slowly as the bomb-bay type doors raised through the water to close and seal the hull. The boy then threw a switch that initiated the extension of a litter rack for catching the torpedo container when released from the Dolphin's grip. Having everything secure, the young crewman went topside.

"Got it?" asked Escara.

"Yeah. It's sleepin' like a baby."

"You rip off any?"

The boy smiled, "Ain't even opened it."

"Take the wheel. And don't smoke no more of that shit till we dock," Escara barked as he left the bridge. "Damn hippy kids," he mumbled. "Goddamn mush brain hippy kids."

Below, Jack Escara checked to insure all the machinery was secure. Seeing the litter rack was set, he decided to release the container and check its contents. As it dropped onto the litter he noticed an addition to the usual sandy brown finish that covered the container. Running the full length of the torpedo was a black stripe that merged into a raven silhouetted by a pale moon. Above the stripe was stenciled the words, LAST HAUL. Escara smiled as he reached out to open the container and inventory its contents.

Topside, the boy had just put another freshly rolled marijuana cigarette between his lips and was searching his pockets for a match eventually coming up with a crumpled book containing only one. He carefully cupped his hands above the wheel, struck the match but never had the opportunity to bring it to the joint. He was suddenly and harshly thrown forward into the wheel of the trawler, crushing his chest. At the same instant a flash of fire engulfed him fully as it did the entire Happy Jack. The explosion spread radically across the surface of the water, its fireball and subsequent smoke challenging the rising sun for supremacy over the morning sea. The Happy Jack and her crew flew apart in thousands of burning pieces, sizzled, then became just so much more man made trash on the bottom of the sea.

Miles away, the Raven's engines surged, her props grabbing that same sea, pushing her south for home waters. Whitemoon handed the binoculars to his steward as he seated himself for breakfast.

"It seems the Happy Jack has just made its last haul," he told his steward.

The steward offered no response.

Whitemoon would have fresh fruit, a small steak, wheat toast and tea for breakfast.

Chapter Seventeen

Carol smoldered, furious, as she paced the length of the motel room. Ramsey simply stood staring out the sliding glass door across Matanzas Bay, hardly noticing the Coast Guard cutter returning after its investigation of the destruction of the trawler Happy Jack. He too was furious, frustrated with his inability to make some kind of sense out of the events and information he had so far discovered. He felt, though he was not sure why, that he was pressed for time, that for whatever reason for the deaths of Fred Dillair, Dillair's wife, and the incident down river at Fort Matanzas, it was critical he make some kind of breakthrough soon. Aside from the name, Nikalow, he had nothing but a gut feeling, an uncomfortable grinding that made his inner panic light flash yet still he couldn't sound the alarm. Not until he had some kind of substantial evidence of a pending threat. He needed Dillair's letter. Theresa had the letter and now she was dead. Whatever it revealed frightened her. Ramsey saw it in her eyes just before she was killed. He felt it to be an extreme paralyzing fear that would leave one not just frightened but hopeless. Dillair wanted to die. 'Whitemoon would get us all,' Dillair said, 'and there's no place to hide.' He wanted Theresa to return to Colorado. The request meant get away, thought Ramsey, far away. Why? Why didn't Dillair get away?

Ramsey thought and rethought everything. It could mean get away from Nikalow, but Nikalow could follow. Distance was not safety. But missiles, thought Ramsey. To be safe from a missile takes distance. Missiles, drugs, Whitemoon, Nikalow. Ramsey simply couldn't put them together. He knew all this but actually knew nothing at all. His jaw tightened as he slammed his foot into a nearby suitcase.

"That's just great. Now you're going to kill my luggage," shouted Carol. "Are you going to tell me what the hell is happening here? I mean, you talk to people and then they get killed. What the hell kind of job is that?"

"Carol, I told you, I'm conducting an investigation. I'm not sure myself what the hell is going on so how can I tell you. Even if I did know I probably couldn't tell you."

Carol stared angrily for a moment then relaxed. "Two heads are better than one," she said softly.

"Your head doesn't have a clearance," Ramsey stated.

"I work in Washington, remember. Baby I feed stuff into computers that would make the President lose his lunch." She moved to Ramsey and put her arms around him, "I'm worried, Ram. I love you and I'm afraid for you."

Ramsey returned her embrace with a long passionate kiss. He suddenly found himself telling her he loved her. They stood silent feeling the moment when a knock came on the door. He glanced out the window and saw Lieutenant Eisen.

"Good morning," greeted Ramsey as he opened the door. "Have you got anything for me?"

"Yes sir. Your packet from Washington."

"Had breakfast?"

"No sir. Didn't have a chance. Captain Downs said you needed this material ASAP," returned Eisen, his surprise at seeing Carol obvious.

Ramsey introduced them. Both silently acknowledged each other.

"Well then, let's see what we have here over some bacon and eggs," suggested Ramsey.

In the restaurant Ramsey slowly read through the papers as he blindly consumed three eggs, bacon, orange juice, toast and coffee. He ignored the grits commonly served with morning southern fair. Eisen sat silent, wanting to discuss the material but was not sure of Carol.

"Is this all that was sent, Lieutenant?" Ramsey asked as he chewed a bite of toast.

"Yes sir."

"From Admiral Peters?"

"Oh, no sir. The Admiral's package never arrived. Captain Downs requested this through another office," Eisen said hesitantly. "Sir, there's something…"

Ramsey saw Eisen's concern over Carol. He smiled, "It's okay, Lieutenant. She's cleared," he lied."

Eisen leaned over to the papers in Ramsey's hands. "In the back, sir. The part about Dillair."

Ramsey flipped the papers over until he reached one that read;

Subject: Dillair, Frederick C., U.S. Navy
Information request - DENIED
Ref: Sec. N47-A3, ADM PTS

"Denied? What the hell is that supposed to mean?" Ramsey questioned angrily.

"We're not sure, sir. Captain Downs rerouted the request to the referred section. There, N47-A3, the Pentagon."

"I know it's the Pentagon. N47 is my section."

"Yes sir," Eisen replied. "But the A3 designates very high security. Even Captain Downs isn't cleared for that information area. We got the same result on a second request to that section."

"So what is ADM PTS?" asked Ramsey as he finished off his coffee.

"Don't you know, sir?" Eisen replied with surprise.

"Should I?"

"That's Admiral Peters. He's the only one who can give access clearance to information in that area."

Carol cleared her throat as if to say, "Well yeah, dumb ass."

"Damn military shorthand," Ramsey mumbled, though his embarrassment was short lived when he realized what Eisen was bringing to his attention. "Now let me get this straight, Lieutenant. We are conducting an investigation as per the orders of Admiral Peters. The only information available to us is in a high security section where it shouldn't be and Admiral Peters won't release it. Is that about right?"

"That's right, sir. It doesn't make sense but that's exactly right. Dillair was, for the most part and as far as we know, just like a million other sailors. His personal files should be available, certainly to us and especially in this case. And get this, the information I gave you at Mayport at the briefing the other day is what I requested and obtained over the phone and when I requested a complete copy of his file be forwarded they agreed then instead of receiving his records, we received a letter stating his records have been lost. They put a tracer on them but you know how that goes. Could be months."

"Lost?"

"Yes sir. Lost. And then denied."

"Did Captain Downs contact the Admiral?"

"He tried, sir," answered Eisen. "Seems the Admiral was unavailable."

"I never did like that son-of-a-bitch," injected Carol.

"Carol, please," came Ramsey. "Not now."

"Well what kind of a boss would send you all the way to Florida for information he's got in his own back pocket?" asked Carol.

Ramsey was about to reprimand her again but remained silent as what she said settled in his mind.

"Maybe Dillair wasn't what we think he was?" questioned Eisen.

"Maybe Peters isn't what we think he is?" questioned Carol. "Maybe he's an absent minded, incapable ass who…"

"Carol," Ramsey scolded.

She turned to Eisen, "Have I ever told you the story about the Navy Grinch who stole Thanksgiving?"

"Will you just put a sock in it," Ramsey stated as he studied the papers. A waitress came to the table with a steaming pot of fresh coffee. Before she could ask if anyone wanted more, Ramsey was holding his cup up for a refill. "What about Whitemoon?" he asked after the waitress moved on.

"Nothing on Whitemoon," answered Eisen. "No military systems, no operations, no person or persons military or civilian. Not that we know of anyway. However the CIA seems to have an interest in Nikalow."

"The CIA?" came a surprised Ramsey as he stirred his coffee.

"Yes sir. But they won't give us anything until we give them some more information. You know the CIA; tight lips, tight asses."

"Good. At least someone is willing to do something. You get back to them. Tell them that Mr. Nikalow, whoever the hell he is, is in St. Augustine, Florida. Tell them he kills people and that he's likely to kill a lot more people if we don't get some information."

"Yes sir." Eisen made a mental note to tell the CIA exactly what Ramsey stated. "Sir, about the Hawk."

"The what?"

"The Hawk missile system."

"Right. Dillair served with a Marine Hawk unit in Vietnam," Ramsey recalled.

"Exactly, sir. Captain Downs thought that was a little strange. You know, that a Navy man would serve with a Marine shore unit of that kind. It's not like he was a CB or SEAL or corpsman and the like."

"A lot of things didn't make sense in Vietnam, Lieutenant."

"Yes sir, well, you wanted to know who we gave the Hawk missile system to."

"That's right."

"Just about everybody, sir. It's basically your everyday surface to air missile. Hell, even the new Vietnamese forces have it. Not that they need it, they have the Russian equivalent."

"I don't doubt that. If they didn't get it in the takeover we probably mailed it to them as an afterthought," Ramsey grinned.

They sat silent for a moment. Each contemplating the possibilities offered by what new information they had or the possibilities and importance of the information they were denied.

"What you need is John Wayne," stated Carol, breaking the silence.

"What," came Ramsey through a gulp of coffee.

"John Wayne. You know, cowboys and Indians, the cavalry, the Duke. John Wayne."

"Carol, what the hell are you talking about?"

"Well, it sounds to me like the bad guys are Indians with this Hawk and Whitemoon and all. Just sounds like you guys need the cavalry. The big Duke on a horse," she laughed.

"It's not funny, Carol," expressed Ramsey. "Be quiet and eat your grits."

"I hate grits."

"So do I," chimed in Eisen.

"I'm glad we all agree on something," said Ramsey. "I wish we could agree on some form of action."

"I know what John Wayne would do," stated Carol.

"What would John Wayne do? Please tell us," Ramsey requested for lack of any other response.

"He would say, damn the Admirals, full speed ahead."

"I'm afraid that would only lead to early retirement," laughed Eisen.

"Maybe not," Ramsey entered seriously. "You said Peters was unavailable. I think I can get around that. I've done it before and I think this occasion warrants doing it again. Meanwhile, you get back to the CIA about Nikalow. I think he's the key and I need that info fast. Also find out what company or companies designed and built the Hawk and what civilian agencies or companies may have access to it. It might take some time but find out how many complete or auxiliary Hawk units have been made and if they can all be accounted for."

"Well now that *could* take some time," winced Eisen in agreement.

"Piece of cake," said Carol.

Ramsey didn't chance to respond. He simply waited for an explanation.

Carol grinned, "I happen to know this computer who is a good friend of mine. And this computer happens to know another computer, et cetera, et cetera."

Ramsey smiled, "Then I guess we're on our way to Washington."

"Oh Ramsey, no. I'm on vacation. You can't do this to me."

"I didn't do it. You just volunteered. It's okay though, baby, I have a feeling we'll be back real soon. But I want to speak to someone before we leave."

"Who?" asked Carol.

"That policeman. The one who was supposed to have dinner with us at Frank's place. What was his name?"

"Steve."

"Yeah," Ramsey recalled as he finished his second cup of coffee. "Lieutenant, I want you to stay here in St. Augustine. Use my room at the motel. I'll call you from Washington before I return. Keep your eyes and ears open for anything strange. Accidental deaths, murders, men from Mars, anything beyond the norm. Whatever you get from the CIA on Nikalow, hold until I return. If it's really hot contact my office at the Pentagon."

Ramsey and Carol exchanged few words on the way to Frank Majors' home. While waiting at a stoplight Ramsey blurted out with laughter, "You know a computer who knows a computer?"

Carol grinned, "Doesn't everybody?"

"Carol, what the hell do you do that would make the President lose his lunch?"

"GSA," she smiled.

"You're kidding. General Services? Are you serious? I mean, I knew you worked at the GSA but…"

"Yep. If you ever want to ruin a politician just come to GSA." She turned to Ramsey seriously, "Do you have any idea how much stationary that man in the Whitehouse uses? It's criminal"

Chapter Eighteen

When Carol and Ramsey pulled into the driveway they found Frank Majors sitting on the floor of his garage. He had his lawn mower dissected and was cursing under his breath as he beat on the housing of the drive mechanism on the front axle. When he saw Ramsey he stood, threw the ratchet at the mower and strolled to the car.

"It's a goddamn conspiracy," he stated seriously, leaning on the car door. "They build these things to make cutting your grass a suburban pastime but when they break down you need a damn engineer to fix them. I think I'll just cover the whole damn place with artificial turf."

"That's a great idea," offered Ramsey as he exited the vehicle. "Then you can sink a few holes and start a miniature golf course."

"You may have something there," Frank laughed. "Don't tell me, let me guess. You guys loved my cookin' so much you're back for more?"

"Maybe in a few days," returned Ramsey. "Actually we're on our way back to Washington."

"Hey Ram, you just got here. You should be able to squeeze a few more days out of the Navy. Hell, you haven't even got a decent tan yet. Come on in and have something to drink and I'll try and change your mind."

"We'll be back in a day or so," Carol said as she looked to Ramsey for confirmation while they entered Frank's kitchen.

"Good," Frank smiled, offering two cold beers to his guests and leading them into the den. "I'll untangle my fishing gear and we'll make a day of it."

"You're on," smiled Ramsey as he flopped on the sofa in the den. "Listen Frank, I wonder if you will do me a favor?"

"Anything for the Navy. Short of enlistment, of course."

"I'd like to ask Steve some questions," Ramsey stated. "Unofficially."

"Something to do with that drug shoot-out on the river?"

"Yeah."

"Do you know what happened last night at the amphitheater?" asked Frank.

"We were there," said Carol.

Frank moved across the room to his favorite easy chair. "You know this town is coming on like the Tet Offensive. People just don't die around here except from old age and credit card shock. You involved in all this?"

"Possibly. Indirectly," replied Ramsey.

"You hear about the trawler?"

"Trawler? No. What about it?"

Frank took a long swig of beer then wiped the perspiration from his face with a dishtowel he had picked up in the kitchen, "A real big explosion took out a trawler this morning a few miles up the coast. That's all I know. Steve may know more and if the trawler is connected."

"I'd like to talk with him today. Can you arrange it?"

Frank made a phone call that brought Steve to the house in fifteen minutes. When he arrived, Ramsey explained who he was but was careful not to reveal too much information. He didn't want local authorities to get involved in the investigation any more than necessary and certainly didn't want to deal with local law enforcement bureaucracy. Steve was comfortable knowing that Ramsey was a good friend of Majors and the questioning was taking place at his home. In addition he was ex-Navy and Ramsey played that card as well.

"What can you tell me about this Marine patrolman who was killed on the river?" asked Ramsey.

"Local boy," answered Steve. "Graduated from high school here a few years before I did actually. Never lived anywhere else except when he was in the Army.

"Have you discovered anything about the incident? Other than what we read in the papers, I mean?"

"Well, at first we thought maybe he came across some drug smugglers and didn't have time to radio for assistance," answered Steve curiously. "But it turns out that he wasn't even on duty. As a matter of fact, he had taken a few days off and the patrol boat he was using wasn't even checked out." Steve hesitated, "I hate to say it but it looks like he was involved in whatever was going down out there. I mean he always was an adventuresome kind of guy, ya know."

"Did anyone find any drugs among the debris?"

"None. Just a bunch of paper in a canvas sack. No ID on the other bodies yet. Probably won't get anything on them anyway. I'd say they're foreigners from down south. Florida is heavy on drug smuggling you know. The whole coast is open and we haven't got the manpower to keep it in check. Not to mention all the legalities and jurisdiction crap we have to put up with."

"I've heard that this Harvey guy said something about someone named Nikalow?" Ramsey leaned into his question with keen interest.

"Yeah, that's right. We tried to question him before he died. Couldn't talk much. He was hurtin' pretty bad. Asked him who did it and all he said was 'Nikalow'. Somebody's name I guess. Only thing we got on this Nikalow is that he buys fish at Jack Escara's seafood place. Now that's a dead end cause Jack blew himself to hell this morning."

"What, you mean the trawler?"

"Yeah, the Happy Jack. Hell, he's only had that boat for six months. Insurance company is goin' to love that." Steve rose from his chair, "Listen, I got to get goin'. Gotta' regulate the pilgrims, ya know."

"Do you think there's a connection between Harvey and this Jack guy?" asked Ramsey.

"I doubt it," Steve answered. "They were tight as fleas growin' up but had a big fight a few years back over some woman. Damn near killed each other. Broke it up myself. Believe me, those boys wouldn't give each other the time of day."

"I appreciate your help, Steve," Ramsey said, extending his hand. "Frank and I are going to do some fishing soon. Why don't you join us?"

"Sure thing but I have to warn you," he pointed to Majors. "That boy there is the worst fisherman in Florida. All you'll catch with him is a sunburn and a big thirst."

"Damn local yocals think they know it all," Majors defended.

Steve laughed and patted him on the back then made his exit. Ramsey turned to the window and stood in silent thought. Majors returned from walking his friend to the door and could see a question on Ramsey's face.

"What is it, Ram? You got that look."

"Didn't you say you met this Harvey, or Stoney as he's called? You said you met him at the beach," questioned Ramsey.

"That's right," answered Majors. "The other day when Blacky drowned. Do you think there's a connection between his death and all this other stuff?"

"I don't know what to think," answered Ramsey. "I'm really hung up on this one. "I'm used to collecting intelligence, not wrangling murder scenarios."

"Listen, buddy, if you need help you let me know. I'm a pretty good investigative reporter, remember?"

"You're a kitchen table writer and retired housewife who can't fix his own lawn mower," joked Ramsey.

"Mother," injected Carol. "And a good one."

"Thanks Carol. I appreciate your defense and support. By the way, I still freelance," he continued, turning to Ramsey. "And I have connections. I was no slouch at the network and there ain't no flies on me yet."

"Does that mean that network applesauce is better than Navy applesauce?"

"Of course not," laughed Majors. "It means if you need information I might be able to help."

"What he needs is John Wayne," entered Carol.

"What I need is a telephone," stated Ramsey.

"Help yourself," Majors offered.

While Ramsey called to make flight reservations at Jacksonville International Airport, Carol and Majors discussed the bizarre facts as she knew them and explained her Duke and cavalry theory by telling him about Hawk and Whitemoon. They laughed it off as Ramsey finished up.

"Our flight departs in a few hours. We've got to go. It's a one hour drive to the airport."

With a promise to return for a day's fishing they were on their way, leaving Majors standing in his garage with his uncooperative lawn mower on which he vengefully dumped the hot end of his beer.

Chapter Nineteen

Ramsey said little during the flight back to Washington, using the time to sort out his newly acquired information and to ponder Admiral Peters' peculiar involvement, or lack thereof. It was late evening when they finally arrived at his Alexandria townhouse after stopping at a restaurant for a leisurely dinner. Carol had insisted on the dinner during which she persuaded Ramsey not to pursue his investigation any further that day but to relax and get a good full night's sleep. He agreed, hoping things would be clearer to him in the morning. She put a pot of coffee on to brew while he entered the shower upstairs. When she finished in the kitchen she went up and slipped into the shower with him. The streaming water pounded the back of Ramsey's neck, hot, relentless, relieving. Carol embraced him and as they stood there in silence under the raining water, his tensions eased, putting everything out of his mind. The missiles, the unexplained murders in a quiet tourist town, the implications of conspiracy and the urgency and desperate impressions all left him. He was slightly aware of a thunderstorm kicking up outside but paid little attention. All he needed now was

Carol. Not even the hiss of the shower reached his ears as he put everything out of his mind. Nor did the sound of the constant pounding on the front door of his townhouse.

Distant thunder sounded and a light rain had begun to fall over the old colonial city as the desperate man pounded at the door. Water mixed with the perspiration on his face as he turned and inspected the dark street in all directions. He was frightened and hoped his Mercedes, parked illegally by a fire hydrant, would not draw attention. Finally he tried the door and finding it unlocked, let himself in. When he closed the door it caused the old glass in the foyer window to rattle. Ramsey had just turned off the shower when the sound of the shaken glass went through the house. He knew the sound. He had planned to have the windows glazed but like other small restoration projects, had put it off. He tensed, putting his fingers to Carol's lips in a motion of silence.

Ramsey slowly opened the shower door, stepped out and pulled a towel off the rack. He moved quietly into the bedroom, wrapped the towel around his waist and from a drawer in an old cherry wood highboy chest near the door, withdrew a .45 automatic, cocked it, then stealthily moved to the top of the stairs. From there he could see, at the base of the stairs, a shadow moving from wall to wall, resulting from the dim lamp near the entrance. He squatted to a near sitting position and slid one step at a time toward the base of the stairs.

Whoever had entered the house was now in the living room. He could see the trail of wet footprints leading from the door as he reached the base of the stairs. Across the dark room a man stood silhouetted by the light of the adjoining kitchen. His back was to Ramsey who now had the .45 extended with both hands to react to any move the intruder might make. Satisfied the man had no options other than a shattered skull, Ramsey inhaled deeply then exhaled, "Don't move or you're dead." His voice was calm and distinct. There was no chance for misinterpretation. Ramsey would kill the man at the slightest move. "Raise your hands slowly," he ordered.

The man responded as ordered. Ramsey squinted, water containing a slight amount of soap found its way into his left eye, irritating a nerve and causing the lower lid to twitch. "Down on your knees," said Ramsey as he rubbed the eye with one hand only making it worse.

The man dropped slowly, wavering slightly. Ramsey's finger instinctively tightened around the trigger.

"Who are you?"

"I have to talk to you," the man responded shakily.

"Who are you?" repeated Ramsey.

"Coggin. Senator Coggin."

Ramsey's mind clicked. It couldn't be a coincidence. "Theresa?" he questioned.

"She... she was my daughter."

Ramsey stood silent. He began to feel the weight of the .45 and releasing one hand but still holding the weapon out with the other, he moved to a nearby lamp and switched it on.

The room filled with light. The senator turned slightly to Ramsey. "I need your help," he said slowly.

"Why?"

"You're investigating Theresa's death."

"Am I?"

"You were there," the Senator stated. "You work for the Admiral."

"I work for the U.S. Navy." Ramsey wiped his eye again with his free hand. "Get up."

The Senator rose and Ramsey quickly frisked him. He found no weapon but did find identification verifying his identity as Senator Albert Wilson Coggin of Colorado. He returned the identification, un-cocked the .45 and motioned for the Senator to be seated.

"I knocked but you didn't answer. So I just came in. I'm sorry. I didn't mean to frighten you."

"Yeah well, the Senate has its privileges but there are limits, you know. It's called the fuckin' constitution. You waltz into my house uninvited and you're very likely to be rolled out." Ramsey suddenly became conscious he was clad only in a wet towel. "If you don't mind Senator, I'd like to put something on. There's fresh coffee in the kitchen. Help yourself. You look like you could use some."

With that, Ramsey returned up the stairs to Carol who was still standing nude in the shower stall. "You can come out now."

She stepped out of the shower and stared at the .45. Ramsey was at one glance both sensually exciting and deadly. He had tossed the towel on the bed and his strong naked body went well with the cold steel of the deadly weapon. There was never any pretense on Ramsey's part. She felt and knew he was capable physically and intellectually to deal with the worst and best life could offer, however this exceptional picture she would store in her mind for future reference.

"Put something on. We have a distinguished guest."

"Who," she questioned.

"Senator Coggin."

He dressed quickly in casual slacks and an old denim shirt that he left unbuttoned and untucked. He was eager to hear what Coggin had to say. When he returned to the Senator he noticed the man had not left his seat. Ramsey went to the kitchen, poured a cup of black coffee and returned to sit across from his uninvited guest.

"Tell me about Theresa," he asked the Senator. "Why would anyone..." He paused, not sure if the Senator was up to the question.

"I know how she died," stated Coggin nervously. "Did you talk to her? Did you see her? Did she know?"

"Know what," asked Ramsey.

The man shifted uneasily in the chair. His hand trembling as he wiped it across his face.

"I spoke with her before she died. She was afraid of something. Desperately afraid," said Ramsey. He sipped his coffee as he inspected the man's desperate manner.

"I thought she was in New York. She was going to start working on one of those television soap operas," Coggin broke down. "My god, how could they..." he said, bringing his hands to his face to hold the tears.

"Who... are they?" asked Ramsey.

Coggin sobbed. Offering no answer.

"Nikalow? Whitemoon?" asked Ramsey.

With the mention of Whitemoon, the Senator looked up quickly. "She knew nothing about this. Hardly anyone knows. They had no right to kill her."

He seemed to babble. Ramsey decided to control the exchange. "Senator, did you know your daughter was married?"

"Married. No," he returned quickly, genuinely surprised.

"Theresa was married to a former Navy man named Frederick Dillair. He was killed a few day before... about a week ago in Florida."

"I didn't know. I haven't talked to her in months."

"Senator," Ramsey's pulse raced as he framed the next question, "What the hell's going on? Who is Whitemoon?"

"They used her to insure my silence. She didn't know anything. She couldn't have known anything."

Just then Carol entered the room and the Senator became extremely nervous. She sat quietly next to Ramsey.

"Who the hell is Whitemoon, Senator?" Ramsey repeated.

"I have everything. The missiles, the Committee. Everything. Can you meet me tonight? I have to be safe. I need protection."

"I'll get you protection. Where and when do you want to meet?"

"I... I don't know."

"How about my office. I'll meet you at the Pentagon and..."

"No!" the Senator stood quickly. "Um... I have a boat at the Corinthian Yacht Club. It's called the Lady Theresa. Can you meet me there in two hours?"

"I'll be there."

Coggin moved nervously to the door. Ramsey stood to see him out but he was already making his exit when he paused and turned to Ramsey, "They're going to..."

At that moment a barrage of automatic gunfire ripped across the townhouse entrance. Carol screamed as Ramsey dove to the floor taking her with him. Bullets tore through the Senator's back, the force sprawling him across the foyer as though he were a puppet and someone had cut his strings. He settled in a lifeless heap in front of Carol who threw her arms across her face and frantically crawled to the protection of the corner of the room. Ramsey desperately rolled to the safety of the opposite wall as the home's entrance and front window was sprayed again with ruthless continuance. Glass, wood splinters and bullets filled the room above them. This time being two weapons, each round, each blast, deadly, deafening and frightening. Carol jerked in fear as they crashed above her then suddenly all went silent. A car door slammed and the sound of squealing tires echoed off the old brick town homes that lined the dark wet street.

Ramsey looked up to see the now dead Senator oozing blood from a series of holes and torn flesh. Carol was curled into the corner; her eyes round with fear. Ramsey sat up, resting his arms on his knees and cursing as he surveyed the damage. Tightly clenched in his right hand was the .45. Carol was surprised to see the weapon, not seeing him take it with him when he left the bedroom. She crawled across the floor to him and he embraced her trembling body as his own fear was quickly replaced by anger. He wanted them now. Whoever they are, where ever they are, he would find them.

Chapter Twenty

The police, the FBI, crime photographers, the coroner, and even the press had wrapped it up and released the crime scene, his home, back to Ramsey with surprising speed. Odd, he thought, almost as though someone wanted as little made of the incident as possible. He wasn't going to argue however and had already found an available 24-hour emergency work crew who were on the job. It seemed you could get just about anything at any time in DC. He hadn't bothered calling the insurance company. How the hell do you explain a dead Senator and machine gun damage to an insurance adjuster, he thought. And to be frank, he just didn't have the time for the delays and petty hassles of the claim process.

Ramsey was buttoning his uniform shirt when the phone rang. Two men replacing the front door and the windows of his bullet torn townhouse worked steadily as he crossed the room and lifted the receiver, "Lightner."

"Commander, this is Admiral Peters. I want you in my office in half an hour." With that short declaration the Admiral abruptly discontinued the call.

Ramsey kept the receiver in hand, pressing and releasing the button for a dial tone. After dialing Carol's number, he glanced over his shoulder to check the progress of the carpenters, estimating they would be on the job for the better part of the day. All of the glass had to be custom fitted, a new door installed and everything painted. Though they said very little as they worked, Ramsey could feel their curiosity with every glance. One worker kept looking at the blood stained floor then at his co-worker. Ramsey offered no explanations. Carol answered the phone.

"Carol?" he asked.

"Yes, Ram."

"How long do you think it will take?"

"She thought a moment, "I'm not sure. I should be finished by noon."

"When you're through, go straight to your apartment. I'll pick you up there."

"Gotcha' Chief," she snapped. "Go straight home. Do not pass go. Do not go to jail."

Ramsey grinned slightly at the monopoly game reference though he wasn't really in the mood. She was one of a kind, he thought, and he would hold on to her. "Be careful," he told her then replaced the receiver.

Ramsey had no intention of going to Admiral Peter's office, not within the hour anyway. He decided to make a little side trip first. Ninety minutes later he stood before a very angry superior.

"You're late!" yelled the Admiral, pointing to a seat.

"Sorry sir. The beltway was backed up," lied Ramsey. He seated himself in one of the two leather chairs that faced the Admiral's desk. Peters rose from behind the desk, turned to the window and stood silent for a long moment. Ramsey watched curiously and noticed the Admiral, though angry, appeared exceptionally calm. But then so did he, all things considered.

"I want to know what the hell's going on," Peters demanded in a low steady voice. Without turning, he continued, "A United States Senator is blown to hell on your door step, his daughter is killed in front of you and hundreds of other people, you've made requests for classified defense information and I haven't received one goddamn written or oral update from you on anything."

Ramsey remained silent. He knew Peters wasn't finished.

"This is the United States Navy, Commander. We have policies and procedures. It's beginning to look like I have no control over my own section and I don't like that very much. Do you understand what I'm saying?" Peters turned to Ramsey; the anger poured from his eyes.

"Yes sir," Ramsey returned. "It's just that I had very little information and…"

"You don't consider the death of a U.S. Senator a reportable item?" interrupted the Admiral as he pointed to the headline of the Washington Post on his desk. "Fill me in Commander. Now."

Ramsey adjusted himself uncomfortably in the chair. "I think we have a conspiracy of some kind, sir. To what degree, I'm not sure."

Peters sat back in his chair, bringing his hands together and resting them in his lap. "No, Lightner," he stated. "What we have is a series of murders, one involving a Naval Intelligence Officer assigned to the Pentagon. To be precise, assigned to me and I'm going to have a tough goddamn time explaining the situation. I need information. So would you enlighten me? Let's start with the Senator."

"Senator Coggin came to my house last night. He wanted information about his daughter's death. There was little I could tell him other than she was married to our dead ex-Navy missile technician. He was in bad shape, emotionally broken up. So I made arrangements to meet him again at a more convenient time."

"What about his daughter? Why would anyone kill her?"

"To keep the lid on the Senator. To play it safe. To cover up whatever Dillair was involved in. There are a number of possibilities, sir."

"Missiles?"

"I'm not sure, sir. I need more time." Ramsey was holding back. He wasn't sure why but felt it necessary. Instincts, he told himself. Trust your instincts.

"We haven't got time, Lightner. I have to come up with some explanations fast. For the chiefs." Peters was also concerned about the news media. He knew they would get to him before the day ended and as usual he could pacify them with some kind of bullshit but could he satisfy the few special readers that worried him most. "I want a full report on my desk in two hours. Everything from day one. Understood?"

Ramsey rose, acknowledged the order and started from the room.

"Lightner," the Admiral called. "The news media. No statements without my approval."

Ramsey turned to find the Admiral again staring out the window. He stared briefly at the man's posture. Something was different. It was something odd, a feeling he couldn't immediately recognize reminding him of those old school days when everyone would be punished for some violation committed by only one person. You had to take it gracefully even though you had no idea what had happened. You shared the guilt and the punishment.

Ramsey's office was not much more than a cube containing the basic necessities of his trade. The metal desk was standard issue and the chair, gray and uncomfortable, was like thousands of others throughout the great Navy machine. As he settled heavily into it a brown envelope setting on top of his IN box caught his eye. He pulled it out, glanced at the routing slip then turned it over.

Across the face of the envelope was hand written:

CMDR R. LIGHTNER, A-47

Written below, in the same handwriting but smaller print, was:

Call me. Urgent.
W.W.

Ramsey recognized the initials as those of Captain Wright Watson, a good friend who owed a few favors. He had visited Watson just before making his tardy appointment with the Admiral. The visit was to collect a favor and the favor was in the brown envelope. He punched Wright's extension on the phone. While waiting for an answer he broke the seal of the envelope and withdrew its contents. What he held in his hand were the records of one Frederick Dillair.

"Captain Watson speaking."

"Wright. Ram here."

"Hey, Ram buddy. You got my note."

"Just picked it up," returned Ramsey.

"Hey buddy, listen," Wright said softly and confidentially. "That's a hot little package I sent you. I know you can't tell me what the hell's happening but I read the papers and got a hunch you need this pretty bad."

"You're right, W.W. I need it bad and I'm grateful."

"Ram, buddy, on that package." Wright paused, his silence conveying his concern.

"Don't worry Wright. No one will know how I got it."

"It's not that. The file's not complete. I mean there's stuff missing, ya know. Current stuff. I think the old man is sittin' on it."

"Oh? I haven't read it yet," said Ramsey.

"Anyway, that's the best I can do," Wright concluded. "Be careful, Ram. Cover your ass. Know what I mean?"

"Sure thing," Ramsey returned. "And thanks again."

Ramsey spread the photocopied records across his desk. At a glance he cold see no obvious missing forms. Dillair's

201 file was apparently complete with assorted commendations, citations and all the usual material to be found in a career man's package. Then he began fingering down the assignments Dillair had over the years when he came to an entry designating assignment to the U.S.S. Lucy. A standard entry showing nothing unusual. The Lucy was a missile cruiser; her base was Mayport, Jacksonville. According to Lieutenant Eisen that was Dillair's last duty station however there was a subsequent assignment entered. This entry made reference to orders dated February 7, 1978. This threw Ramsey off track. Eisen said Dillair was given a hardship discharge in 1977.

He quickly started fingering through the stack of orders attached to the 201. Near the bottom of the stack was the copy he was looking for and more. First there were orders awarding Dillair a commission with the rank of Ensign. Another promoting him to Lieutenant and more until he eventually reached the rank of Lieutenant Commander. The later dated 1980. A fast riser thought Ramsey as he flipped back to the 201 cover. Earlier he had only glanced at the name on the file. Now closer scrutiny revealed the rank of Lieutenant Commander. He turned back to the orders concerning Dillair's last assignment not finding a DD214 military separation form but finding instead an assignment to the Pentagon. To be precise, one Lieutenant Commander Frederick Dillair was directly assigned to section A-47 under one Admiral Peters. Ramsey stared in amazement. Why hadn't Peters told him, he wondered. Why play games? The rules were all being broken, not by Ramsey but by Peters. The Admiral, with all his clearly expressed policy and procedures, was either bound by security or using him as bait. Now that I know more, thought Ramsey, I seem to know even less.

Ramsey thought back to his earlier conversation with Peters. He noted the Admiral never mentioned the request for Dillair's records, a request he denied or avoided. He, in fact, never mentioned the Dillair business at all and being this man's death was the instigation of the investigation... Ramsey was unable to draw any reasonable conclusion for the Admiral's behavior. The Admiral was angry, recalled Ramsey. Angry because he was not being informed of the investigation and yet he knew of Theresa's death. Also a newspaper reporting the Senator's death sat on Peter's desk. Ramsey chilled. Peters called him at 0530 hours. Before the media got wind of the story and before that special edition reached the street. As far as Peters should have known Ramsey was still in Florida.

He hastily stuffed the file back into the envelope, grabbed his briefcase from the floor and slammed it on top of the desk, wincing as he remembered it contained the loaded .45. He then checked to insure the safety was on, tossed the files in the case and slammed it shut.

Leaving the Pentagon, he wondered what W.W. meant when he said there was missing material from the file. Indeed there must have been something somewhere to account for nine years of military service. Ramsey's own file showed at least a record of TDY entries showing brief notations of temporary assignments whenever he traveled. This was standard records procedure and should have been noted somewhere in Dillair's file. Missing records aside, Ramsey now knew Dillair had been part of the team, a very silent team member, and now a very dead silent team member. As he exited the building he cultivated the thought that perhaps Peters' exclusion of information from Ramsey was intended to protect him. The less he knew the least likely the chance he would come to harm. Ramsey was angry and confused. He had gone too far to be excluded from anything. Someone had invaded his home and nearly killed Carol. They nearly killed him and left a bloody public servant dead on his living room floor. Peters' policies and procedures could go to hell. Now Ramsey was out for blood.

He tossed the briefcase on the passenger seat as he slid into the royal blue Datsun Z car, automatically injecting and turning the ignition key. The radial tires noisily grabbed the hot parking lot surface when he angrily threw the car into gear. He glanced at his watch, it was nearly 0900 and there was time to make a stop at the Corinthian Yacht Club before picking up Carol. He considered going to Senator Coggin's home but quickly dismissed the thought. Officially or otherwise he would not be a welcomed guest at this time and there would also most likely be members of the press. He would confine his present search to the boat and if he found nothing then someone else would have to search the house. He hoped whatever it was the Senator had would be on the Lady Theresa. It was unlikely he would keep it at home and endanger his family. The worse case scenario being of course that the good Senator kept everything in his head; which at present was just plain inaccessible.

The Corinthian Yacht Club was nearly deserted. The boats rocked lazily, water lapping their hulls, nylon lines echoing as they slapped against hollow aluminum masts. As Ramsey walked the length of the dock big band music of the 1940's drifted lightly from an old houseboat. When he passed it by an old woman sporting a long neck Lowenbrau beer smiled up at him. Ramsey returned the smile and noticed she was reading one of those supermarket tabloids. He supposed it was her idea of the ideal retirement and, he laughed to himself, maybe she was right.

He was about to turn and ask the old woman where the Lady Theresa was birthed when he spotted the Senator's boat at the end of the dock. He noticed the boat was showing its age, an old thirty-two foot Owens obviously used and rigged primarily for fishing. It was the kind of boat only a mother could love, or a true fisherman who didn't give a shit about impressing the yacht club crowd. Ramsey jumped on board causing the boat to rock slightly and tug at its mooring lines. He glanced around, satisfied no one was watching, then forced the cabin hatch open and went below where he systematically searched the boat finding nothing. Frustrated, he leaned against a window above the small sink, noticing it was crusted with age and neglect. Ramsey felt ridiculous searching for something but not knowing what. As he turned to leave he angrily slammed the door to the head shut and charts, loosely replaced after his hasty search, fell to the deck. He cursed under his breath and bent to retrieve them, then pausing thoughtfully, he picked them up, moved to the table and unrolled one then another. They were standard charts, mostly of the Potomac River and the Chesapeake Bay. He then rolled out a series of maps darted with red circles, each circle containing the notation, *HAWK*.

"Bingo," he said aloud. The maps were of the east and west coasts of the United States. Closer inspection revealed no exact locations but Ramsey noticed that all were within what he guessed to be the Hawk's range of fire to coastal military installations. One, he noticed, was just west of the St. Johns River near Green Cove Springs, Florida, within range of all three Naval installations at Jacksonville. St. Augustine was but a few miles east. He noticed another within range of the new Trident Submarine Base at Kings Bay, Georgia. All the sites were numbered consecutively beginning on the west coast and ending with Florida. In addition they were all checked off with the exception of the one near St. Augustine at Green Cove Springs, which was also the last in the numbered series.

Now Ramsey was painting a picture, a picture that frightened the hell out of him. A picture he now knew demanded immediate action.

Chapter Twenty One

Within hours Ramsey and Carol were on a flight south. Having a brief layover in Atlanta, they decided to review her findings over drinks at an airport lounge.

"The principle developer and contractor for the Hawk Missile System is the Raytheon Corporation," she informed Ramsey as she unfolded the computer printout. "These figures show cost, dates, production stats, et cetera. This was the easy stuff. Now here is where I had to do a little razzle dazzle." She flipped a page to reveal an unintelligible mass of brevities, numbers and dates. "This is the status of every little screw and bugger in every Hawk System ever made. I want you to know I charge extra for this."

"What's all this mean?" questioned Ramsey.

"Beats the hell out of me, baby. I just pushed the buttons. It's up to you military brains to make sense of it all. There is something here that is readable though and you're going to love me for it."

"Don't tell me, let me guess," returned Ramsey. "John Wayne's phone number."

"Nope," she smiled as she flipped the page. "Stock holders. Everyone who ever held stock in every company that's ever been involved in the Hawk System development, production or maintenance."

"Christ Carol, it's endless."

"What can I say? One pushes a button and behold, computer cornucopia."

"Why should government computers have stockholder information?"

"Who said they do," she smiled slyly. "Ask me no questions and I'll tell you no lies. Besides, I don't believe you're that naïve. It doesn't have to be *on* government computers. The government only needs to have access, known or otherwise. And intelligence is all about access, right."

"Your learning fast and no, I'm not naïve. Just surprised."

"You shouldn't be. We all know you guys have files on people that reveal their toilet habits so what's so big about stockholders? Especially where defense contracts are concerned."

Ramsey smiled, "Sometimes toilet habits are more important than your average corporate info."

"Yeah, I'm sure that will come in handy when the world is drowning in bull shit."

"There's little chance of that," said Ramsey as he studied the print out. "Now all we need is an expert on government brevity codes. If there is such a thing. Not to mention a Wall Street wizard who knows stockholders like Rona Barrett knows Hollywood. Neither of which we have time for just now."

"I'm sorry. I was only trying to help."

"That's all right. It may be useful. I'll look this over on the plane." Ramsey sipped his drink, deep in thought.

"Ram, why don't you get out of it," said Carol seriously. "Out of the investigation and out of the Navy."

"Are you serious?"

"Yes. Very serious. I love you." She took his drink and set it aside then took his hand in hers. "I'm frightened. My god, people are dying on your doorstep. It's like some unofficial war or something. It's insane."

"You're right. It is a war and it is insane."

"Who cares? Let Peters handle it. Let Eisen handle it or anybody else. Why does it have to be you?"

Ramsey asked the waitress for a fresh drink then turned to Carol, "I want you out of this. I want you to go back to Washington."

"No way," she stated quickly.

Ramsey knew better than to argue with her. She was too stubborn. "Then at least stay with Frank when we get back to St. Augustine. He'll understand. You'll be safer there."

She nodded agreement then Ramsey, surprising himself, told her he loved her, would leave the Navy when he finished this assignment and without difficulty, stated they would be married. Carol, for the first time since they had met, was speechless. At least for a moment.

"Can we live in St. Augustine?"

"Anywhere."

"The honeymoon. Where can we take the honeymoon?"

"Anywhere," answered Ramsey. "Anywhere and everywhere."

They were laughing now as they strolled through the airport terminal to board their next flight, Carol making plans and deluging Ramsey with possibilities for the honeymoon, their future home and future professions. Ramsey simply agreeing happily with everything she suggested, knowing she would change her mind with each day. It was so easy. Putting all the death, the implications of conspiracy, the urgency, and the questions, the continuous questions, out of his mind. He envied the hundreds of people he saw throughout the air terminal who simply hurried from point A to point B. They were so lucky to be ignorant of the world as he knew it. Traveling for business or pleasure, profit or pastime. They simply existed, not caring about anything other than their own little world and he saw them with envy and anger. He weighed the price of their delightful ignorance through flashed memories of war, of classic legends of the bloody sacrifices of entire generations and the unprecedented ingenuity of industry and science. They are never aware of the constant turmoil, the subtle struggle to maintain and control the extremes of a supposedly civilized free-world society. He wondered, should he survive this current obscenity, if he and Carol could truly be happy. He likened it to being a doctor. How does a doctor find beauty and strength in the human body after a lifetime of treating its frailties, abuses and diseases? How can he and Carol exist in a world constantly abusing itself? In a society obsessed with destruction. He would depend on her, he would have to, he thought. He would use her joy, her body and her humor. She was stronger than he in many ways, ways she would never be aware of and to a degree he would never be able to explain. She would keep his sanity and blanket the nightmares. She had become an important part of him now, a necessity, and with all this, an undeserved luxury.

Upon arriving at Jacksonville International Ramsey rented a civilian automobile; having decided the Navy vehicle, which he left there the previous day, would be too obvious. It would be, he thought uneasily, an easy target. From there they drove Interstate 95 south to St. Augustine. Along the way very little was said. He drove solemnly, seriously approaching and contemplating the happenings and facts that occurred over the past twenty-four hours.

Their first stop was Frank Majors' house. Ramsey brought him up to speed and his friend Majors took Carol in without hesitation. Soon after, the two boys came into the house and they and Carol began making plans to attend the Days In Spain Festival. She agreed to stay with the boys while Ramsey and Majors checked in with Eisen.

"Commander, boy, am I glad to see you. Admiral Peters has been calling Mayport. He's hot as hell. I think you're in deep shit, sir."

"Let's get inside," Ramsey said to Eisen at the motel door. "I want to get out of this uniform. Have you got anything new?"

"Yes sir. Plenty," the junior officer replied. He waited until they were in the room to continue. "The CIA is all excited. They want to send a man down. I told them no. It would jeopardize our situation."

"Good," approved Ramsey.

"It seems our man Nikalow is a Russian agent."

"What?"

"A Russian, sir. The CIA lost track of him six months ago and they are hot to pick up on him again. My guess is they will send someone here anyway but at least they'll have to find him the hard way and stay out of our way while they're doing it."

"What kind of Russian agent?"

"They weren't too clear on that. My impression was that he's a two sided coin or very independent. They want him because he's open game. They weren't very secretive but they have their own damn language and it was a little tough to politely tell them to fuck off. Um, if you know what I mean, sir."

Majors was pacing around the motel room and finally settled in a chair by the patio door. He observed a large yacht as it maneuvered for mooring at the city dock.

"That's all I need, a damn Russian. As if this whole show wasn't complicated and screwed up enough," said Ram as he angrily changed into civilian clothes. "Tell me more."

"Admiral Peters wants you back in Washington *now*. Captain Downs said to give him the word and he'll stall the Admiral for you. Apparently they have a history and the Captain doesn't care for the Admiral very much."

"Good. Tell him to stall. Anything else?"

"Yeah! That's it! Now I remember." The statement came from across the room from Frank Majors who was standing and pointing at the yacht across the Matanzas.

"What?" asked Ramsey, turning to the window.

"Raven! Raven Industries!"

"Frank, what the hell are you talking about?"

"You remember when Carol was joking about John Wayne and the Indians?"

Both Ramsey and Eisen nodded remembrance.

"Whitemoon. Whitemoon stuck in my mind. I've been playing with it in my mind ever since you left. Now I remember. I used to do financial news for the New York Times. It was back in the sixties. I covered a story once about this eccentric rich industrialist who went bananas and started buying up the state of Pennsylvania. They finally had to put him on hold. He claimed it was his heritage and if he couldn't buy it he and his brothers would take it back the way they had lost it. Said he was an Indian Chief. He combined all his wealth, holdings and businesses, which was quite a lot, and formed Raven Industries. And get this, he changed his name to Whitemoon."

"Are you sure?" Ramsey questioned.

"I don't remember all the particulars but I'm sure, yes. I remember because it was soon after that I went with the network and was assigned to Vietnam."

Ramsey then remembered the computer printout and quickly went through it, scanning it with his finger. He finally froze, "There. There it is. Raven Industries. Damn, he had controlling interests in most all of the companies that subcontracted to Raytheon."

Eisen and Majors hovered over the printouts taking in the data as Ramsey pointed to the pertinent listings.

"He must have built his own arsenal of Hawks. Look at this," he said excitedly as he removed the maps he had found on Senator Coggin's boat and showed them to the two men.

"These are most likely all of Whitemoon's Hawk launch sites. Each within range of a major coastal military installation."

"But the Hawk is just a surface to air system. A SAM for air defense," stated Eisen, partially questioning, thinking aloud.

"You're forgetting Whitemoon's resources. All he needs is the missile. No tracking units or radar. A simple missile, preprogrammed mobile units, easily hidden and with modifications they could be fully remote. He doesn't even need personnel on the sites."

"Ramsey," Majors hesitated. "Are they nuclear?"

Ramsey turned to the window, "They must be. I don't know how the hell he did it but they must be. He must have converted for nukes. Nothing else would be worth this kind of effort." Ramsey chilled. "That crazy bastard is going to start a nuclear war." He turned to Eisen, "Jesus Christ, our military wasn't designed to fight crazies like him and the intelligence people have obviously failed."

"We've got to do something, Ram. And we've got to do it fast," stated Majors. His manner was controlled but inside he grew desperately frightened.

"Eisen, get these maps to Captain Downs. Fill him in and tell him to personally jet them to Washington. And Eisen, by no means is Admiral Peters to be informed of anything. I can't explain why but that's important."

"Yes sir. I'm on my way. Oh, there's something else, sir. You have an appointment tonight. An anonymous caller left a message for you to meet him at the Conch House Lounge at nine."

"That's it?"

"That's it, sir. That's the whole message."

Ramsey turned to the window after Eisen left for Mayport. "Nice boat," he stated.

"Yeah," agreed Majors. "That's what made me remember Whitemoon."

"What do you mean?"

"The yacht. She's named *Raven*. She just pulled in."

Ramsey's eyes were on the classic old yacht though his mind raced with the pending crisis. He thought how lucky the passengers of the yacht were. Their only concern was pleasure and travel. He was now burdened with the task of stopping a demented man and a bizarre conspiracy. Part of him now wished he was the village idiot.

Onboard the Raven, Whitemoon's man was briefing him on the recent interest in their affairs. Whitemoon had begun his own investigation when he suspected a third party involvement in the incident at Fort Matanzas. Now he listened with interest about a Navy Intelligence Officer and his woman companion.

Chapter Twenty Two

Ramsey checked his watch as he walked along the planking of the sea wall that ran the length of the shore of the small motel marina complex. His anonymous caller said nine. Ramsey was early. He moved slowly, checking out the area, getting a feel for the environment in case of an emergency. Situations such as these seemed to sharpen his senses, his awareness of places and things otherwise ignored. Not because of the fear, he had learned long ago to deal with that. It was selfish interest. His ability to somehow condense what should have been slow enjoyable experiences into brief remembrances. It was as though he were being cheated of the luxuries of travel even though he traveled a great deal. It was always business, Navy business, government business. Always a problem, always a situation to be scrutinized, analyzed and then reported and acted on. Just sponging up information like a damn robot. He never really cared one way or the other but kept himself removed from the people involved. He was there but he wasn't. Now he felt the difference, the responsibility. He was being drawn in, unable to remain the mechanical specialist he was trained to be. He felt the urgency, the fear, and the strain because now it affected people he knew and loved and cared about.

The Conch House Marina was a pleasant place with an easy warm breeze tossing the palm trees along the shore of a quiet island inlet. Ramsey moved cautiously past a palm thatched seafood restaurant at the base of the dock. Here people dined, drank and laughed by candlelight. He had become more defensive, more aware of danger since the incident of the Senator's death. Now walking from the restaurant over the water out the few hundred feet of dock to the marina's Conch House Lounge he felt like a duck in a carnival shooting gallery. For comfort he remembered the .45 holstered under his jacket.

The lounge was an octagonal wood structure resting above the water on concrete stilts. Subtle old pre-synthetic jazz mixed with laughter drifted from within, filling the moonlit marina with a relaxed tropical island atmosphere. He paused at the gangplank leading to the lounge's old brass doors. The place was small, too small to meet someone and remain unnoticed by other patrons. In addition it was crowded with a constant turnover of patrons. It made Ramsey uneasy.

Two college age girls, drinks in hand, exited the lounge and were making their way noisily down the gangplank, one depending heavily on a thick rope for guidance. The other, a little more inebriated, tripped on a cross board and fell into Ramsey's arms. She dropped her drink, the plastic cup rolling off the dock and into the water to float off with the tide. She made no apologies but simply smiled seductively as she righted herself and slid out of his arms.

"Any time," smiled Ramsey as he watched them sway away along the dock. For some reason he briefly questioned his decision to marry Carol then told himself to get used to the idea of putting such ideas out of his mind.

Turning back, he glanced past the lounge to the marina. An assortment of small boats, yachts, houseboats and schooners rocked slightly with the tide. The tranquil scene should have relaxed him but failed to as he remembered his task at hand, the rendezvous, a risky meeting with an unknown caller. It was a foolish stupid move but necessary. He needed information and he needed this possibly dangerous meeting. Hell, he told himself, he needed anything that would help him understand the insanity of his newly discovered threat.

Ramsey entered the lounge, found a small table near a wall and sat facing the entrance. Still he felt insecure. The structure sported three large sliding glass doors, all of which were open. He uncomfortably sipped his drink, bourbon strait up, took in the nautical décor and casually inspected the people around him. Ten minutes passed. Fifteen. A half hour. A ships bell clock sounded above the music. Ramsey checked his watch and decided it was time to get out.

Ramsey departed the lounge and had walked half the distance of the dock to shore when he spied someone standing in the shadows beneath the roof of the restaurant. Nearby oil burning torches on poles extended from the sand among the palms. One near the dock flared up with the breeze, lighting the partially hidden figure well enough for Ramsey to see him draw an automatic pistol. He stopped cold and reached for his .45 hearing at that same moment a voice behind him.

"Here, Commander. I'm here and you're going to die."

The voice was cold, clear and deep. It was accented. Russian!

Ramsey had no other option but to quickly hurdle the waist high restraining dock rail for the safety of the water below. To his surprise and disappointment however the water was only thigh deep. The tide was out and so was Ramsey's time, he thought, as he raised the .45 in hopes of getting off the first shot. Unfortunately it would be a blind shot as he realized his eyes were blurred, burning from the salt water, having been drenched as the result of his clumsy desperate exit off the dock. Suddenly a foolish thought ran through his mind, that he wouldn't have time to cry before he died. The flashing thought made him angry and snapped him back.

Nikalow smiled down sadistically, his arm extended, finger tightening on the trigger of his weapon. As the moonlit killer came to focus in Ramsey's eyes he heard an automatic pistol rip through the tranquil marina. Three shots, POP POP POP! Nikalow jerked back against the rail, firing into the water, missing Ramsey by inches, then fell to the dock in disbelief, clutching his blood covered chest. Ramsey turned quickly. He had not fired the shots. It was the dark figure near the restaurant. The man with the automatic pistol moved carefully from the shadows. Ramsey, not sure of the situation, cautiously aimed his .45.

"Are you okay, Commander Lightner?" asked the man standing over Nikalow's bleeding body, his hand trembling as he tucked away the weapon.

Ramsey said nothing, remaining still, wet and confused. He stared first at the strange black man who was apparently as frightened as he, then at the blood trickling through the boards of the dock and twirling through the water with the movement of the tide. He watched it come to him and ooze around him as though Nikalow were still reaching out to kill him.

"I'm sorry, Commander. I didn't know he was aware of our meeting," the man spoke slowly, drudgingly.

"Who is he?" questioned Ramsey.

"He is David Nikalow, a Russian agent, a Committee agent, a killer for profit and pleasure. He was a control problem and a fool.

"And just who the hell are you?"

People were slowly coming out of the restaurant and from the lounge.

"I'm not sure any more, Commander. That's why I'm here."

Ramsey climbed out of the water and onto the dock. He tried to ignore the stares of the crowd as he stood dripping,

.45 in hand. "You saved my life and I appreciate it but I'm really not in the mood for riddles. Now, who the hell are you and why did you want to meet me here?"

"My name is Richard Cannon. I work for the Committee and I could care less about your life. I'm here because this whole damn world is about to go up in smoke. You've got to stop it." He paused, looking down at Nikalow. "I'm tired, Lightner. I want out but there is nowhere to go, no way out for me. I'm a dead man."

Ramsey searched the man's eyes. They revealed, as he said, a tired and hopeless individual. Ramsey had seen those eyes before, in Vietnam. It was a look men got when they lost reality or their desire and expectancy for life. They called it *the thousand-yard stare.* "I think we could use a drink," suggested Ramsey.

"Yes," Cannon agreed. "Why not."

Ramsey reached out to escort Cannon to the restaurant. As they turned two shots rang out sending Cannon sprawling spastically into the crowd. People screamed in panic as they tried to scatter within the limited confines of the long four foot wide dock. Ramsey turned, dropping to his knees, extending the .45 with both hands. He fired repeatedly and all five shots found their mark. He then rose slowly and with the weapon still extended walked to Nikalow's body. He bent, retrieved the dead man's pistol, and wished aloud, "Go ahead, move you Russian bastard. Move so I can kill you again." Ramsey's pulse raced as a flurry of excitement invaded his emotions. The excitement he had felt in the war, the kind that bred survivors. It was almost pleasing, forcing him to deny the feeling as he had years before in Vietnam. Ramsey turned his attentions to Cannon who lay heaving in pain.

"Lightner!" said Cannon as he grabbed Ramsey's shirt and held on desperately. "They have it all, Lightner. But that's not good enough. They use people like you and me... and... Whitemoon." He jerked in pain as Ramsey checked the wounds in his side. Losing fast, he reverted to the street dialect of his youth, "We ain't nothin' man!" he laughed. "They gonna' fuck dis whole world, man. And you..." The wounds burned and the pain raced with every throbbing heartbeat. He pulled Ramsey closer, "You don't trust nobody, man. You hear me? Nobody!"

Ramsey looked to the crowd. He was about to send someone for medical aid when he heard an approaching siren. When he looked back Cannon was dead. He pried the dead man's clutching bloody fist from his shirt, removed his jacket and covered Cannon's face then removed Cannon's pistol and wallet. He turned and viewed Nikalow's corpse. It never changes, he thought, the way dead men lose their dignity as if to prove they were after all just another animal. For those few moments Ramsey was back in Southeast Asia and for those few moments he almost wished he was.

Chapter Twenty Three

At that same moment in the oval office of the President, Captain Downs paced uneasily, the Secretary of Defense leaned back in a chair, lighting his pipe for the third time, and Admiral Everest F. Bartlett, the Navy's top ranking man, stood staring out the window into the Washington night, the light and movement of the city hardly filtering into his mind. He was angry. Downs had broken the chain of command to present a pending crisis. Crisis or not, to a career man like Bartlett, Navy Chief of Staff, you don't circumvent the system or break the rules. It was bad for the Navy and set precedent and looked like a breakdown in *his* Navy. This Captain Downs would pay, thought Admiral Bartlett. If just cause were not presented, he would pay big time.

The door opened abruptly and the President, dressed in formal evening attire and ignoring everyone in the room, went directly to his desk where he slid open a drawer, rummaged through it, then slammed it shut. "Well Shit. Jack you got a cigarette?" he asked of the Secretary of Defense.

Admiral Bartlett came from the window and seated himself on a sofa. The President did the same opposite him as the rest of the company joined them. Secretary of Defense,

Jack Hollingsworth withdrew a pack of cigarettes from inside his jacket and tossed it to the President who caught it easily, withdrew one and was about to toss the pack back when Hollingsworth advised, "You better keep them, Mr. President. You're going to need them." Hollingsworth's comment came with a smile though he was very serious.

"Damn woman thinks I quit. Isn't that a joke? The President has to hide in his office to smoke a cigarette." He lit the cigarette, tossed the lighter on a nearby table and settled back. "Maybe I should take up cigars," he smiled. "Might get some political mileage. You know, that good ole' boy father image everybody misses so much now days. Or Havanas. I'll smoke Fidel's Havanas. That should get a rise, keep the boys in the press offices busy for awhile, huh Jack?"

Admiral Bartlett adjusted himself further into his seat. He was uncomfortable as usual. Not that he often visited the Whitehouse but when he did he disapproved, or at least was disappointed in the casual manner in which the President conducted business. Bartlett was the product of military academies from age five, the old schools where square meals and stiff collars were sometimes more important than a man's knowledge and ability. 'If you can't master the chicken shit how can you master the world?' he would say. In turn, the President often contended, 'If he took his job too seriously he would have gone nuts his first month in office'. In truth, the President was indeed a serious and capable man. His exterior, light hearted and casual, was a tool. He discovered early in his political career that he needed an edge. He needed time for thought and deliberation, a luxury that seemed to no longer exist in today's world due to the immediacy of the media and the public's McDonalds mentality. Decisions, the right ones, come slow, the result of a deliberate process and he had a *do it right the first time* policy which worked well, causing him to sometimes be referred to as that *damn old slow New Englander*. A handle he accepted as a compliment. He made few mistakes as a politician and intended to make fewer as President yet he was the first to admit the office was too much for one man, creating uncomfortable dependencies. He staffed his cabinet with care and his personal staff with long trusted political servants. To the dismay of party loyalists he showed no political favor and some went so far as to claim once he was elected he showed no party preference. It was all part of his charm, a beautiful spider web catching and holding the trust of the entire system. With people like Admiral Bartlett this worked well, insuring their overconfidence, lowering their defenses and while they did, the non-threatening *old slow New Englander* slid right on into the Whitehouse.

"Okay boys, now what's so hot that I have to miss another boring state dinner?"

"I seriously feel this needs further investigation, Mr. President," Admiral Bartlett volunteered. "We may be overreacting?"

"Hell, Admiral. Don't you think I should know what it is we're overreacting to?" the President said, snuffing out the cigarette. "That's what you boys are supposed to do, isn't it? Sort of sort things out a little before they get to me. Hell, I'm just the finger in the dike here. Up to you folks to find the hole."

"I think perhaps Captain Downs should present the problem, Mr. President," entered Hollingsworth.

"Welcome to my humble home, Captain. Now what have we got here? More drugs on our floating airports or did one of our new generation gunners get pregnant?"

Captain Downs smiled, recognizing the Presidents technique as his own. "It's obvious you were an Army man, Mr. President, or you would know that our modern Navy smooth legged seamen are all stewards exclusively on call to their commanders. For their own benefit, of course."

The President laughed, "Don't let my wife hear you say that, Captain. She's a damn feminist. Gets votes though."

Admiral Bartlett squirmed with disapproval at the observance of their informality; which happened to catch the sharp eye of the President. "Don't despair, Admiral," said the President. "It's just good ole' boy talk. And we're a dying breed if it's any comfort."

"Mr. President," Downs continued. "I believe we have a crisis."

"I'm listening, Captain," said a now very serious Commander and Chief.

"As the result of a current investigation by Navy Intelligence, we have discovered there is at this moment a series of missile sites with nuclear capability, each located near our coastal military installations and all except one poised and ready for assault."

"On American soil?" asked the President, sitting up with surprise.

"They're American made missiles, sir. Installed by an American citizen for the purpose of initiating a nuclear war."

"Jesus Christ! You mean... Am I to understand we now have to contend with nuclear threat from our own citizens?"

"One citizen, sir. Or at least one group led by a single man. It's ironic, sir, but he's an Indian Chief." With that said, Downs backed off a little to let the President absorb the information and to add urgency to what he was about to reveal.

The President turned to Jack Hollingsworth for confirmation.

"It all checks out, Mr. President," said the Secretary of Defense. "And it gets better."

"Better," stated the President. "I hope the hell that's a play on words, Jack."

"There's a Russian element, sir," Downs continued. "Though we're not sure why. Could be they're trying to prevent this man's success or they could be involved in a supportive way. The fact is we have little time to deal with the situation."

"How much time?"

"We're not sure. Our agent in place feels everything will pop soon after the completion of a final site in Florida. He's there now."

"Do we know where these missiles are?"

"We have the general locations of each site but they are converted STA missiles, mobile and easily hidden. We can start a search but there may not be time. Our best defense is foreknowledge. We'll have to blow them out of the air," Downs hesitated. "If we can catch them in time. My guess is they're designed for an airburst. Depending on the type of warhead, they could be highly destructive or simply temporarily immobilizing with minimum nuclear capacity but enough to throw our defense system into action against the Russians."

"Why would the Russians want a war now?" asked Admiral Bartlett.

"It's a unique situation," Hollingsworth observed. "As I understand it, this Whitemoon character wants Indian justice. He's supposed to be off his rocker. If we believe that then we have to deal with this internally by holding back our defense system and military and of course, inform Moscow of the situation. Then they could take advantage of the situation by launching an actual attack. If Whitemoon succeeds, it could paralyze our strategic coastal areas fully or partially. These are critical. It would be too tempting a situation for the Russians not to take advantage. If this guy only wants to start a war and then stand by and watch, he sure as hell covered all the bases. Um...No pun intended."

"He certainly knows how to ruin a state dinner doesn't he Admiral?" It was the President's way of getting a response from a man he wasn't fond of but in which he held great confidence.

"We have the capability to destroy the missiles in flight," Admiral Bartlett stated. "We will have to alert every concerned area, ground most all civilian aircraft, maintain heavy radar coverage and stay airborne constantly until this thing is over. It could be a hell of a strain and drain if we have to drag it out too long."

The President leaned back in his seat, lit another cigarette and remained silent. He appeared not to be concerned.

Hollingsworth emptied his pipe in a nearby ashtray. His many years of involvement with this man before he entered office taught him patience was a virtue. He knew a decision was being made at that moment and action would be taken within the hour. That's the way this man handled critical matters. The President would call his crisis team together, throw a couple of senior Senators into the mix, play them all for all they were worth and leave them thinking the ultimate action decision was theirs. After all, he was a politician, a diplomat, and a genius manipulator.

"Captain Downs, where do you call home?" the President smiled.

"Got a little farm in Vermont," Downs returned. "I retire in a few weeks."

"Well, you certainly have a way of going out with a bang."

Both men laughed. Admiral Bartlett cringed.

"You've done well, Captain. I trust you will keep me informed? I want everything, including after action reports. That is if we're around to write them when all this is over."

"Certainly, Mr. President," agreed Captain Downs.

"Jack, I want you to roust the Chief of Staff and you and the Admiral fill him in. Initiate actions to stop those damn missiles, whatever it takes, then call the team together so we can play with this thing. And for Christ sakes keep it quiet. If the folks in Moscow and the press don't know I'm sure as hell not going to tell them. Not yet anyway."

They all rose and the President escorted Captain Downs to the door. "Hope I'm in time for dessert. Wasn't to keen on dinner anyway. Some damn thing I couldn't even pronounce."

Bartlett stood, amazed. The world was near destruction and the President was going back for dessert.

As the President was making his exit he turned back to Admiral Bartlett and his Secretary of Defense, "I'll be back in one hour gentlemen," he stated seriously. "By then I expect our entire defense mechanism to be in motion." He then looked to Hollingsworth, "Jack, I want you to get with State and have them play with the Russians and find out where they are on this thing. Take it slow, be careful but don't bullshit. We haven't the time to be touchy feely." Turning away they could here him mumble, "Probably some damn dessert I can't pronounce either."

Chapter Twenty Four

It was early morning, soon after Whitemoon had eaten breakfast when he gave instructions concerning what was to be done about the Navy investigator. He didn't know the extent of Commander Lightner's findings or why he was involved. He did however consider him a threat and an obstacle to the final phase of his plan and the less than forty-eight hour countdown to its activation. Short of murder, Lightner would have to be dealt with in a way that would insure Whitemoon of the time he needed. He had conceived an action that he was confident would accomplish his goal to buy time and silence from the Navy man. Leaving this responsibility to his people, he decided he would inspect the last and final launch site in Green Cove Springs, then return to the safety of his island. From there he would with ease and great satisfaction touch off the spark designed to let loose the raging forces of destruction held by the great powers of the world. He knew of these forces because he helped build them. He knew how the expert minds of war designed the controlled destruction of other nations. How they too would be destroyed but were satisfied with their percentages and degrees of survival. How they ridiculously predicted survival rates and recovery standards as though humanity were on a game board. To win the game, regardless, even if only one playing piece was left standing. Whatever the outcome, thought Whitemoon, I will have my justice. Like a child who would rather lose his toy than share it, Whitemoon, having been denied his heritage and his son, would destroy his world.

Carol and the boys had formed a relationship even their father now envied. She was a natural entertainer who loved children, especially boys, and had no difficulty establishing a line of communication on their level. In turn they picked up on her personal humorous quirks and were already challenging their father with newfound sarcasm. Majors didn't mind. It was a pleasant change and their spirits were high, creating a diversion to the looming peril of which he had recently become aware. He hadn't told Carol of the drastic situation or the events of the previous evening at the Conch House. Ramsey insisted she not know. Instead, Majors sent them off to the festival.

"Okay, you animals, lets keep it together," Carol directed as she and the boys twisted their way through the festival crowd. They'd started at the north end of St. George Street in the Antigua section of town by the old city gates and were working their way south discovering along the way the festival was something of a Mardi Gras affair but on a much smaller and more subtle scale.

It was a warm bright day, promising to grow hotter as the sun reached its noon peak. An inland breeze carried the scent of fresh baked bread, meat pies and sausage rolls from the Spanish Bakery. Other pleasant aromas from the carnival-like street venders drifted through the air as well. Above a water wheel in an old wooden mill house, a single guitar player crooned story songs to entertain tavern patrons but his music was suddenly overcome by screams as a handful of Pirates made up of Junior Jaycees abducted a young girl tourist off the street. Her freedom would cost someone a dollar. Witnessing this, an inspired young Chris grew a conspiratorial smile and started for one of the abductors but Carol quickly snatched him back by the collar, "Don't get any ideas kid," she said, letting him know she was aware of his intent to have her captured.

They continued taking in the offerings of the day, sampling everything from Spanish ice cream and meat pies to white chocolate. Local people and merchants roamed the narrow streets in sixteenth century attire while a quartet of musicians pumped out authentic Spanish compositions of the same period followed by costumed dancers. Laughter echoed off the stucco and coquina walls down the street and out into the small town as the dancers snatched embarrassed onlookers who, red faced, joined in the light-footed steps and twirls. It was then Carol noticed the sour faced man when he rudely refused to dance. His eyes caught Carol's. They were piercing and serious. She dismissed it and she and the boys moved on.

It had taken nearly an hour for them to roam half a block of the busy festivities. They were inspecting the window of an antique toy shop when she and Tony realized they'd lost young Chris. Backtracking, they finally found him smiling devilishly as he sat posing for a street artist. The artist's cartoon caricature sketch brought out the devil even more. Chris, having to sit perfectly still for the artist, requested Carol to bend over.

"That man keeps staring at me," he told her.

"Of course he's staring," Carol returned. "He's drawing your picture."

"No, not him," Chris shifted his eyes. "That man over there. The mean looking one."

Carol casually glanced in the direction of Chris' eyes where she saw, leaning against a wall across the street, the same hard eyed man who rudely stared at her earlier. She got the impression he was out of his element, perhaps a foreigner, and it wasn't difficult for her to conclude this man was not enjoying himself. He continued to eye them without inhibition, his interest apparent. Then another man joined him. This man turned, looked at Carol then entered into conversation with his companion. As they spoke, Hard Eyes raised his arm to extract a cigarette from his shirt pocket. When he did, Carol saw a pistol tucked behind his belt and she quickly turned back to Chris.

"See, I told ya," said Chris. "That guy's weird."

Carol snatched the caricature from the easel, surprising the artist. "That's great," she said. "You're really good. How much do I owe you?"

"But I'm not finished," he protested, surprised.

"Yes you are," she returned. "We're in a hurry. How much?"

"Five Bucks."

"Here." She shoved the five-dollar bill in his hand. "You really are good. Thank you."

Carol snatched Chris from his perch on the posing stool and started down the street. Tony tagged behind, digging into a crumpled bag for some final chips of white chocolate.

"Come on kiddo! We gotta' make tracks," she called back.

Tony quickened his step, still digging. "What's the hurry?"

"Don't ask. Just stick with me. Close."

"Hey. The picture's not finished," Chris said, striding to keep pace with Carol.

She stopped, brought the boys together and told them secretly, "You know that weird guy who was staring at you?"

They nodded.

"Well, he has a gun and I think he's after us."

"Oh shit!" exclaimed Tony.

"Hey, watch your damn language, kid," she scolded. "Now listen. We're going to boogie down this street and get away from those guys so keep your cool and stick with me."

She looked between and past the boys to see the two men approaching then turned and the three of them began winding through the crowd. As they quickened their pace the shadowing men, confirming Carol's suspicions, matched it. She looked over her shoulder repeatedly to check their progress, discovering the man with the hard eyes was now carrying a deadly serious glare and decided to close the distance.

Carol was now feeling the heat of the day and their current situation made it seem even hotter. The sun was straight up burning down on pink tourists who seemed out of uniform in poorly matched shorts and synthetic shirts, their cameras dangling from wide Indian print straps. The entire scene was becoming surreal, much like a slow motion dream that she had to endure because of the restrictive pace of the boys. She gasped when suddenly from behind a wall two Spanish Conquistadors clashed swords. They moved into the street yelling challenges, swords ringing. Chris slowed to watch and Carol yanked him on. The dueling Spaniards blocked the street, giving her and the boys a gain. Hard Eyes impatiently moved about the increasing crowd searching for a break in the combat. When it didn't come he and his companion forced their way through, pushing one of the young fencers against a wall. "Boos" of disapproval came from the crowd which was ignored by the abusive men as they trotted on.

By now Carol and the boys had reached the plaza, an open park area that hosted the festival's arts and crafts show. Behind them, a block away, their pursuers came at a trot.

"Safety in numbers," Carol mumbled, edging the boys into the dense crowd. Somewhere among the maze of people, paintings and handmade trinkets she heard and then saw a banjo picker serenading babies on a makeshift blanketed grass nursery. They quickly squeezed through intellectual discussions on wood sculptures then bounced from a wondering fat man to nearly running over a skinny senior citizen.

"Excuse me, ma'am," Tony winced as the old woman's breast pushed into his face.

The plaza was jammed with people. Walking was difficult, running impossible.

"Hurry!" Carol instructed as they skidded through the crowd, then her heart raced when she realized they had again lost young Chris. She glanced back to see Hard Eyes had discovered them and was directing his partner to take an alternate route. They were closing in. Carol desperately searched in every direction for Chris. Tony looked at her pleadingly as he tolerated a reprimand from the little old woman.

"Where's Chris!" she cried.

"Over here," yelled Chris.

The boy had gone ahead and was waiting for them to catch up. Carol, relieved, grabbed Tony and started for Chris when Hard Eyes' partner stepped out to cut them off. They froze as he raised a hand to the pistol in his belt.

"Oh shit!" Tony exclaimed, drawing the man's glance. Carol took advantage of the brief distraction by solidly planting a knee in his groin. He rolled to the ground, tumbling a wall of oil paintings, sending people scattering as the line of canvases crashed and fell.

"Run Chris!" Carol yelled as they leaped forward to a full sprint through the market place and emerged into the street. Tires screeched as drivers slammed on their brakes to avoid hitting them. All three ran full out as they made a turn down a narrow brick way, Avilles Street. With no festival activities taking place there it was nearly deserted except for a horse drawn carriage containing a driver and two tourists. When Carol turned to look back she stumbled and fell over the old deeply rutted brick. The boys stopped and turned, unaware the carriage was coming up behind them. They were more concerned with what was behind Carol.

"Carol! Look out!" screamed Tony, raising his arm to point behind her. The motion spooked the approaching horse which jumped and twisted from side to side, jerking the carriage. The driver lost control and the horse bolted forward.

Carol turned to discover Hard Eyes had found her. He reached out but she desperately fought him off, turned to run but fell again as he grabbed her from behind.

When the horse and carriage heaved forward the boys jumped aside and jammed themselves flat against the wall of the nearest building to avoid being run down. The powerful uncontrolled animal began running the carriage in varied directions, up over the curb and into buildings, the axle hubs grinding away at the stucco. A girl in the back screamed and the now wide-eyed carriage driver lost the reins and tumbled back over his seat into the laps of his passengers. The horse now ran completely wild, its heavy hoofs and the steel rimmed wheels of the carriage pounding the bricks below. Carol turned from her struggle with Hard Eyes to see the oncoming horse and carriage. She screamed then desperately clawed her way clear. Hard Eyes leaped to the opposite side of the street and fell striking his head, leaving him stunned.

At that same moment his companion came running from the main street, unaware of the oncoming danger. He was struck full on by the wild-eyed horse and thrown into an oncoming car. The horse continued into traffic causing a chain collision, crossed the street, then stopped and reared when faced head on by the side of a parked van.

The boys ran to Carol's aid and helped her up. She looked to see Hard Eyes was dazed and struggling to regain himself. He recovered and the chase resumed with Hard Eyes stumbling after them, leaving his companion sprawled across the curb with a fractured spine. His long strides gained on them as they ran a twisted path along deserted narrow lanes and shaded old back streets barely wide enough for a single automobile. Carol was winded but fit enough to continue, however the boys had trouble keeping up, especially young Chris. He was frightened and the continued chase on lonely streets supported his fear. Carol slowed and reached for his hand. Close behind, Hard Eyes stopped and extended his weapon. Seeing this, she slowed to a stop and brought the small boy behind her for protection. Tony backed slowly to the side of the street. Hard Eyes, walking toward them, held the site of his weapon on Carol. The Spanish moss in the old oaks that stretched over and shaded the walls and rustic wood and iron fences along the street swayed with the breeze. No other sound filled the air except for the heavy breathing of the tired runners and the deadly metallic click as the man's sweaty thumb forced back the hammer of his gun.

Chapter Twenty Five

Ramsey paced the motel room impatiently waiting for the phone to ring. Across the bay some kind of commotion caught his eye. He slid open the glass door and took a seat on the hot sunny patio. Sitting there, looking across the bay to the old city, he felt as though he were somewhere in Europe. He tried to place the feeling, eventually narrowing it down to the Mediterranean. It was the climate, he thought, and the architecture, the boats, and of course that bridge. Somehow it reminded him of the Grand Prix, or Monaco, though he didn't know why because he had never been there. It was a collective vision born of movies, TV and magazines. Perhaps it was the four spires or the many flags waving from the old gas style light poles. They lined the bridge like centurions, from the two lions on its west end to the foot of the east end where the bridge met his motel.

It was a pleasant town. He could understand why Frank would settle here but then Frank Majors was a writer who could live anywhere. What would an ex-Navy intelligence man do in a tourist town? Carol insisted they live here. For her this place was love at first sight. She was impulsive, he thought, then he smiled. She was also intelligent and determined. If they were together it would work anywhere. Life, Ramsey concluded, was people not places. He lit a cigarette and leaned back into the vinyl webbed aluminum chair casually admiring the classic lines of an old Trumpy yacht as it broke away from the city dock and maneuvered to the bridge. Ramsey remembered the old Trumpy line, built in Annapolis, Maryland, they were mostly custom designed for the bays and inland waters of the east coast. This one was a big old girl, a hundred feet plus easy, and must have a deeper hull than most, he thought, it was heading out to sea. "Good luck old girl," he said, casually saluting as the Raven cruised through the raised bridge. The yacht's horn returned the tribute, echoing across the bay and the bridge's centurions, the flags, stood at attention. Ramsey envied her captain and found himself wishing they could trade places.

The telephone finally rang. It was Eisen.

"Commander, I have that information for you."

"I'm listening."

"Here goes," said Eisen. "Richard Arthur Cannon. Born, Detroit, August 7, 1943. High school grad, honor student. Drafted U.S. Army, 1963. Discharged 1968, honorable. Two tours in Vietnam, one in Germany, the rest stateside. Airborne Special Forces, heavily decorated. Was a language instructor in the states and Germany, also attended college while in service. Continued college after discharge, UCLA, but didn't finish. He was involved in the racial activities of the sixties. Was considered by some to be an extreme radical, by others to be one of the more intelligent activists in a category with Martin Luther King. I've got some good stuff here. National magazines, newspapers, et cetera. He was among the media's choices to be one of the black Americans destined for political success but he faded out in the early seventies. Not much on him after that. He never married. Was an only child. No surviving parents. It looks like a dead end Commander."

"What about organizations, his profession, associations?"

"Nothing, sir. He was a loner. We tried a social security trace but it showed no employment since his military discharge. He had a combat sustained disability but the checks came back undelivered. The VA closed his file six years ago."

Ramsey perked up, "Is there a chance this guy really wasn't Cannon?"

"No sir. The prints checked out, so did the teeth," Eisen answered. "I ran a check with the airlines. This may be something. Cannon flew down here from Washington. We've also discovered he had an interesting passport. For the past two years he has traveled most of the free world plus one trip to Russia, one to China and a couple to the middle east. Said he was a business consultant. It was probably a front. There was no company listed. Do you think he worked for Whitemoon?"

"I don't know," answered Ramsey. "He said something about the *Committee*. Said they used people like him and me and Whitemoon. It could have been a dying man's hysteric rambling but he sounds like the kind of person who would choose his words thoughtfully. He was a linguist, remember? It's just an impression but I think this whole mess goes further than Whitemoon. I'm not sure how or where but I can feel it."

"Here's something else that may interest you, sir," added Eisen. "Captain Downs has returned from Washington. Says to tell you that everything is under control from the Whitehouse. He also says he did some checking and discovered that Admiral Peters and Senator Coggin ran in the same social circles. Admiral Peters, by the way, is on an emergency leave and can't be reached. The Chief of Staff is hot on this whole thing and coming down heavy on your area of the Pentagon. Um, Commander," Eisen hesitated. "The Captain said for you to be very careful, not to trust anyone."

"That's funny," Ramsey returned. "Cannon said the same thing before he died. Dying men rarely lie. I wish I knew what the hell he was talking about."

"Commander, it sounds like you need help. We've got some good men here. I can have them there within the hour."

"I'm not sure what we're up against, Lieutenant. Put them on hold and I'll yell if I need help. Is there anything else?"

"Captain Downs is out right now, sir, but he wants to talk to you."

"I've got some things to check out here. Tell the Captain I'll get to him as soon as possible." Ramsey discontinued the conversation. As he replaced the phone the sound of a siren came from across the Matanzas and in through the open patio door. He walked out and looked across to where the commotion near the old market place in the center of town now featured police cars and an emergency medical truck. He wondered if Carol and the boys were in the crowd of onlookers or were somewhere else in the festival area, maybe having lunch at that Monk's place where they dined their first day in the old city. Wherever they were, he thought, knowing Carol he was sure they were having a good time.

Chapter Twenty Six

The aircraft carrier U.S.S. Saratoga was twenty miles off the northeast coast of Florida, returning home to Mayport after six months of duty on the Mediterranean. Below decks a good many crewmen, instead of jawing about their homecoming priorities, entered high gear and rushed to performed their duties. Others however, moaned and bitched, a few violently, because they had just been informed they would not dock at Mayport as scheduled. Games they thought, drills, Navy bullshit. Instead the *Sara* had been ordered to hold off the coast and turned into the wind. Her flight deck buzzed with action as she entered combat mode and aircraft were readied for launch.

Lieutenant James Meredith, call sign *Disco*, young, medium height, fair-haired and not long out of the Academy, chewed his lower lip as he left the briefing room. He was not alone in his tense anticipation of what would take place in the air over Jacksonville, a city of seven hundred thousand plus people and three naval installations. This was the real deal, he thought, and it was difficult for him to believe that his first real action would take place over U.S. soil.

The briefing was a shock, as cold and hard as the gray steel of the Sara herself. They were not told everything, only the necessary data concerning the missiles and that they would be supported by ground action and radar. The missiles were assumed to be configured for an air burst and may not be detected by radar in time for anti-missile defense due to the short range factor. In a nutshell, each squadron, each pilot, would ride a tight circular razor blade around their designated area of protection and take immediate aggressive action without hesitation to destroy anything that flew. Like a carousel, thought Meredith, or wagons in a circle waiting for the Indians to attack. He could not have known the irony of his thoughts.

On a high school football field two teenage boys were readying their homemade ultra-light motorized glider. They were proud of their new machine. It could take off and land on a dime and its swept wing design gave it an edge on speed without compromising maneuverability.

The boys were gloating, eager and gutsy, ready to test fly this second machine. Their first ultra-light did all it was designed to do but its pilot did a little too much and the machine was lost when the State Police impounded it after buzzing the Gator Bowl during the Florida/Georgia classic. Now the boys snickered confidently as they prepared a revenge flight. Indeed, they had even christened the aircraft *Sweet Revenge*.

"I'm gonna' fly this sucker right over City Hall," the young pilot threatened proudly.

"Right up the mayor's ass," his companion laughed. "Now remember, get plenty of altitude then cut her off and glide her a while 'cause you ain't got enough gas to make it there and back."

"No sweat, man" smiled the amateur pilot as he dawned his circa 1918 leather flight hat and goggles. "Piece of cake."

In flight less than an hour, Lieutenant James Meredith sweated nervously as he fingered the powerful hydraulics of the F-14 Tomcat. Like other pilots in the Skybird Squadron he searched the sky intensely, his rear seat companion constantly checking the aircraft's radar. And like the others, he had difficulty putting the questions out of his mind. He was defending U.S. soil from missile attack. Why? Who? If they succeeded in stopping them, what would happen next? What if they couldn't stop them? Could he live with the failure? Would he live at all? Survive the blast? Were these missiles an advance to something else, that ultimate horror which had evolved over the years into something that no longer served the defense of a free world but instead dominated and threatened? Has the *no win* scenario begun?

He struggled to put all this aside. Concentrate, he told himself. Focus. Do your job. It's the Army/Navy game in Memorial Stadium on that cool fall day in beautiful old Annapolis. The stadium is packed with dark blue uniforms and white hats. They chant in unison as you do your part. You're a halfback again, blocking, leading that power play that sends the fullback in for the winning touchdown. Suddenly Meredith sees seven hundred thousand faces. They line the streets of Jacksonville and stare up at him pleading, "Don't let us die, Jimmy boy! Help us! Protect us, Jimmy boy! Don't let us die!"

With his stomach twisting, tightening, he flashes to his girl. She's down there somewhere doing what she does each day at the bank. She must be thinking of him, probably even planning to get off early because she was going to meet him at Cecil Field when the squadron flew in ahead of the ship. What was it she wanted to do tonight at that place on the water? Now he remembered. It was...

"Radar contact! Bogie, coordinates..."

"I've got it! Skybird Three to Skybird Leader. I've got bogie. Going down now," Meredith snapped as he rolled the

Tomcat left. The F-14's wings swept back and he felt the exciting surge of power as the aircraft moved to intercept.

"Locking on bogie," Meredith stated mechanically. Damn, he thought, it's inside. It's inside the perimeter. How the hell did it get inside?

His target was not visible but it was there, miles away, beneath the clouds.

"I've got him. I've got a lock. I've got him. Now!" His heart raced as his own missile burned away from beneath him.

As Meredith's missile sought out its target another F-14 soared in down through the clouds at a lower altitude to confirm the hit.

"Oh shit!" came the squadron leader. "Jesus Christ!"

Above the St. Johns River the small engine purred steadily as the young pilot played his ultra-light left then right to take in the view. He had just buzzed the Gator Bowl and set his sights on the big glass tower. He used the wind, circling, soaring, his adrenalin surging. He felt as though his lungs were going to burst as he breathed the fantasy of free flight. Yeah, this is great! This is better than sex, he thought, somehow forgetting he'd never had sex. Barely touching the clouds now, he was about to cut the engine, bank left into a three-sixty then right and circle the towering glassy Independent Life Building, the tallest in the state, when he heard the deep cat-like scream of the F-14. It came out of nowhere, powerful, impressive, steadily arching wide until it leveled toward him far in the distance. Someday, thought the young delinquent flyer, I'm going to pilot one of those bad mothers.

He angled the ultra-light for descent and at that same moment Meredith's missile shot through the clouds dead on target. For all the boy knew, it was a shadow, a seagull, anything. His eyes saw it but his mind never had time to identify it. The explosion ripped the frail ultra-light and its pilot apart as easily as a stick of dynamite in a paper bag but with hardly enough debris to resemble confetti as it fell above the riverbank parking lot.

On the upper levels of the nearby Independent Life Building, clean, quiet, stylish offices became chaotic as massive heavy plates of tinted glass shattered inward from the blast. Pieces of missile and glass penetrated furniture, walls, computers, and of course, people. Some screamed, some simply sat in amazement. Those unlucky few who had the choice space with the scenic river view had been sliced like prime steak, their bodies separated, their eyes still open and minds still wondering.

"Base, this is Skybird Leader. Be advised, we have just killed civilian ultra-light. Expect heavy damage to Independent Building. Many friendly casualties probable."

"Skybird Leader. We copy. Be advised, all flights maintain. Repeat, all flights maintain."

"Roger, Base. That's affirmative," acknowledged the squadron leader. "Disco, how goes it?"

Meridith, having listened to Skybird Leader's dark assessment to base was frozen, his stomach turning.

"James, my man. You okay?"

Meredith hesitated then finally responded, "Affirmative, Skybird Leader. We... we're okay here."

"Maintain status Skybirds," ordered the squadron leader. "This party ain't over."

In the Whitehouse situation room the reaction over the Jacksonville incident was matter of fact. This was the second such incident in as many hours, the first taking place near San Diego when an Air force fighter took out a small civilian jet. There were near incidents as well over Norfolk and Philadelphia.

All civilian aircraft in these critical areas which just about included the entire east and west coasts had been notified and either grounded or diverted under various guises in order to avoid such incidents. Some were simply escorted away without explanation.

The Whitehouse war room reeked of anxiety as military brass and cabinet members paced the floor, listened to situation reports and monitored the large screen that seemed to give the pending crisis all the character of some elaborate fictitious video game. Subordinates manipulated computer consoles, answered telephones and were already processing that data necessary for effective retaliation against whatever part of the globe was unfortunate enough to get sucked into the limited or unlimited exchange of destruction.

Unlike the others, the President took the news differently as he prepared for a possible quick exit to a safer control situation on Air Force One.

"Our defenses have been operative but a few hours and we're already killing civilians," stated the Secretary of Defense. "This is going to get real messy when the media picks up on it."

"Look at it this way, Jack," the President returned. "Maybe they were democrats. No, no, excuse me gentlemen. I apologize. That was in poor taste," he quickly conceded.

"There'll be more such incidents if this drags out. We'll rotate the aircraft but those boys are wired pretty tight," said the Secretary.

"Wouldn't you be?" the President suggested. "Hell, Jack, we're dealing with American air space here. They're defending their own back yard. Let's hope these incidents are the worst that happens. And when this thing is over, if we succeed, I want the pilots involved in those incidents brought here to me. I know the military and I know Capitol Hill. I don't want those boys caught up in any aftermath bullshit witch hunt that'll ruin their careers and their lives. They're doing what we trained them to do and what we asked them to do and doing it well. Damn it, I'll personally assign them all to Air Force One if I have to."

"What about the media?" the Secretary questioned. "We're going to have to deal with them soon. They know we're on alert and they're already banging down the doors."

"They can eat it," returned the President. "We have a job to do and we can't do it if we have to cater to the press. If we tell the truth they'll blow it out of proportion, panic the whole damn country and screw up our defense efforts. It's like inviting this Whitemoon character to the Whitehouse for a briefing. If we feed them bits and pieces in an effort to control the situation they'll come up with all kinds of speculative crap. Look what they did to Carter with the Iranian thing. They had the poor guy so twisted he didn't know whether to fart or tinkle."

"There'll be leaks and they'll be persistent," observed the Secretary. "Like you said, this is U.S. air space. You can't shoot people out of the sky and not be noticed. Our coastal bases are closed tight, our military worldwide is jacked up. Hell, it's not exactly a small covert operation."

"Just let it go for a while. If it starts to look bad then get me on the phone to all the media heavies. If they won't put a hold on it for security and operational purposes then they'll suffer the consequences. Hell, I'll padlock the press if I have too. There's no justification in the freedom of the press if it jeopardizes the survival of the people. It's just plain common sense. Damn Jack, you know how I feel about this. I refuse to let the media hold prominence in the decision process of this administration. It hasn't yet and it isn't going to. Especially not now. Not in a crisis. I'll not have some damn uninformed pin-head calling the shots on the tube like we're playing a fuckin' football game or something."

"It could hurt you politically."

"The only thing that can hurt me is me not doing my job. If I have to cater to the press I have to neglect the duties of this office to do so. The press will just have to wait. They're people like the rest of this nation's population. What the hell good is the six o'clock news if its audience is dead and buried. I don't want to talk about this any further, Jack. When the time comes put John on the phone. He knows what to do. That's why he's my Press Secretary." The President turned to John Crews who sat listening patiently from the far side of the room. He continued, "John, if they won't sit on it until the time is right, well then, you let them know that I'll come down hard. National security and all that."

The President rose as if to emphasize his words, "The people have a right to know but they also have a right to live as well as know why things get screwed up. And the media's no innocent party to national screw ups. Hell this country has fought wars because of an ambitious greedy press but it won't hold prominence here. Not today. Even if it cost me a second term." He settled himself as he moved across the room to study the big board. He wasn't really angry but simply driving home the point, making things clear. It was also his way of waiting, dealing with the stress.

Everyone understood. The media would not be mentioned again throughout the crisis. Not even John Crews, the Press Secretary, would bring up the subject. Instead he would take notes, keep a record of each action, each statement, each victory and each mistake. When all was done, he would run it down with the President and unless something was compromising to the national security or simply in poor taste the press would get it all. It was better that way, the President affirmed. Less room for error and media manipulation. The people get the whole picture, nothing's out of context, everything's in perspective and they can draw their own conclusions.

Of course few of the President's people agreed with his media philosophy, however they had to tolerate it along with many other idealistic concepts of public service held by the Chief Executive. After all, it somehow worked and it put them in the Whitehouse. His staff, Commander Ramsey Lightner and the President most of all would later realize the true value and benefits of what was to become a need to know operation.

"Now folks, since our military is obviously doing their job, let's do ours and start formulating some communications to keep the international situation in check. I'm sure they've heard some rumbles by now and are getting a little antsy," came the President as he retrieved a legal pad and handed it to Alison Garner, the Secretary of State. "Allison, I want your feedback on this. I know it's short and doesn't answer all their questions but hell, I don't have time to play games with the Russians. You know what I mean?"

Allison Garner was a damn genius which is exactly why she was Secretary of State. She never missed a trick, the President would say, she could deal with the big picture, focus on the small picture, was diplomatic, totally loyal, had total recall, and could rationalize a dirty pig in a white wedding dress. What impressed the President most of all about her resume when he selected her for the job wasn't her sheepskins from Stanford and Harvard but the fact she helped pay for them by working summers as a smoke jumper in Oregon. She was tough and everyone knew it. In confidential circles the President was often fond of saying, "Don't fuck with me. I know Allison Garner."

A quick read of the Presidents copy and Secretary Garner formulated her opinion. "Considering the time element involved, Mr. President, I think it's quite to the point." she said. "I couldn't have said it better myself unless I knew a Russian language phrase equal to *shit or get off the pot.*"

"My sentiments exactly," smiled the President. "Now, get that off to the Russian Premier and then get down to business with our world neighbors on a need to know basis. Can you imagine what the British will do with this? I can hear it now: 'The Colonies still at war with the Indians.' How embarrassing," he laughed then became exceptionally serious. "I only hope we're all still here tomorrow to suffer such embarrassment. And... I sincerely hope the Russian Premier is the man I judge him to be."

Chapter Twenty Seven

Ramsey was impatiently pacing around the swimming pool of the small motel, eagerly anticipating the arrival of Captain Downs and Lieutenant Eisen. He had long ago outgrown the confines of the motel room and decided he needed more light and space. Downs had called him nearly forty minutes earlier informing him the information they had would allow them to finally take some action against Whitemoon. He also filled him in on what was happening in Washington and of the incident in the air over Jacksonville.

At last, thought Ramsey, at last we can do something. We can at least try and become the aggressor, force something to happen, maybe zero in on this Whitemoon guy. Anything at all was better than sitting around playing with the assorted riddles of information and watching the clock.

The gray Navy vehicle pulled into the motel parking lot and Ramsey was at its side before Eisen had even turned off the engine.

"What have you got?" Ramsey questioned eagerly.

"Green Cove Springs," returned Eisen.

"There's an old Naval Air Station there," entered Captain Downs. "It was a bee hive of military activity during World War II but is deserted now. It was bought by Raven Industries eight years ago, supposedly for conversion to an industrial park. We matched it against the Senator's map and the locations are the same. I've called up a SEAL team. They're ready to fly in on our command."

"We've got to get in there and see what we're up against. Is it guarded?" asked Ramsey.

"Don't know," replied Eisen. "There must be some form of security. My team will check it out from the air. Whatever is there, I'm sure my boys can handle it."

"Your boys?"

"Commander, if all I did was push papers I'd go out of my mind," smiled Eisen. "My SEAL team is the best in the fleet."

"And I suppose they play softball every weekend, too," Ramsey said, expressing his contempt for the puffed pride of the peacetime service.

"They're combat vets, Commander. All of them," stated Eisen, failing to tell him they did actually play softball on the weekends.

"And you?"

"Lieutenant Eisen put in three years with the Army's Airborne Rangers before he came to us, Commander," assured Captain Downs. "He's the best of two services."

"I apologize, Lieutenant," Ramsey winced. "It's just that you look too young... I mean, I should have known better."

"Lied to the Army about my age, sir. No need to apologize."

Downs chuckled, "Now that you two love each other it's time to get down to business. We need to get in there fast. Our whole defense system is so uptight right now it could go off without the help of our rogue Indian Chief."

Eisen was spreading a map over the hood of the car when Frank Majors screeched his station wagon to a stop behind them.

"Jesus Christ, Ram! They've got the kids and Carol!" he stated as he jumped from the vehicle. He was desperate and angry. "My kids, damn it!"

"Frank, what the hell are you talking about?"

"It's that Whitemoon bastard. Here, read this."

Ramsey took the note. Sick desperation crawled through him as he read.

To Commander Ramsey Lightner, U.S. Navy

I firmly suggest you and your company cease current investigation immediately. Do not further endanger children and girl. Their lives are in you hands.

Whitemoon

"I thought they were at the festival," said Majors. "My God, Ram. The kids!"

Captain Downs turned away from the two men. He knew Ramsey had a difficult situation. He also knew he had a more important engagement. Ramsey would have to make a tough decision, finding his lover and his friend's children or trying to prevent global genocide, meaning of course, he actually had no choice. Downs could not face Majors when the decision was made. He also knew if the Commander made the wrong decision he would have to pull rank and override him. The life of the country was at stake and as cruel as it was, the opportunity cost of the lives of one woman and two children were minimal.

Eisen looked to Ramsey, they were using up precious time.

Ramsey searched Frank Majors' eyes and his own soul. He could find no words, no expression to ease the desperation. He quickly turned to Eisen, "Put your boys in the air. We've got work to do."

"My God, Ram!" Majors stated intensely as he pulled Ramsey to him."

"Frank... it's already begun. I can't stop it." Ramsey reached desperately for something to say, "But I think I know where they are. We're going there now." He actually had no idea where Whitemoon had taken his captives or if they were still alive. He simply had to say something to give Frank Majors hope. "Is your wagon gassed up?" he asked Majors.

A hesitant, "Yes," came from Majors. "I'm going with you."

"Sir." Eisen offered up a silent protest.

Ramsey looked at Eisen then back to Majors, "Do you know the old Naval Air Station at Green Cove Springs?"

"Yes," answered Majors.

"Then get us there. Fast!"

Eisen quickly transferred his and Ramsey's combat gear from the Navy car to Majors' wagon.

"I'll stay here," said Downs. "I'm too old for this sort of thing. Mr. Majors can use my gear. I'll contact the team and get them off then arrange a direct line to Washington so you can get out what critical info you discover. Remember, we need to know more about the missiles, their launch time, the type of warheads. I'll monitor the choppers but you contact me as soon as you get something."

A half hour later the wagon sped across the long concrete bridge that spanned the St. Johns River a few miles east of the old navy base. At that same moment two UH-1H helicopters cruised low over the river from the north. They pulled up then banked right, buzzing Frank Majors' station wagon.

"That's the team!" Eisen shouted over the whopping roar of the choppers. He quickly grabbed a field radio and started setting up a cautious attack plan.

Ramsey eyed Majors curiously as he loaded his .45 automatic then Eisen passed two M-16's over the seat. Ramsey locked an ammo clip in one, locked and loaded, switched on the safety, and laid it across Majors' lap. "You remember how to use it?"

"Yeah," Majors returned, removing one hand from the wheel to adjust the weapon. "We're almost there."

"Team reports no activity except around an aircraft hanger near the main runway," came Eisen. "Heavy overgrowth on most structures. One vehicle near the gate and a truck by the hanger," he continued to interpret from the static filled radio, "The choppers will hold off beyond the trees near the base out of sound and sight. They'll hang back until we call them in." He tapped Majors on the shoulder, "How far are we from the gate?"

"Um... maybe a quarter mile."

"Good. Drop me here," ordered Eisen.

Majors slowed to a stop near the overgrown chain-link fence. "Meet you at the gate," said Eisen as he exited the vehicle, hopped a ditch and cleared the fence in a matter of seconds, his movements sure and cat-like.

Ramsey and Majors continued along the road. The sight beyond the fence was eerie. Old weathered barracks sat empty, windows cracked, broken or missing. The buildings were faded and flaked with peeling paint, some boarded up, most overgrown with large leafy vines. Poles extended into the air above the two-story structures, their wires long since stripped for the copper. Water pipes and utility lines ran through the air from building to building. Once heavily wrapped with insulation that same insulation now hung torn and ragged, dangling from the pipes mixed with vines and gray Spanish moss. Beyond the buildings could be seen the wide expanses of weedy runways and open land, bordered by tall long-needle pines.

As they approached the gate, Ramsey searched the area for people, memorizing the layout. He saw one guard seated in a small glass enclosed hut. A metal swing pipe barricaded the one lane entrance.

"I can ram it," said Majors.

"No," replied Ramsey. "Go on down the road to give Eisen a little time then turn around and pull up to the guard hut," he said as he covered their gear in the back seat.

A few minutes later the wagon returned to the gate.

"Just pull up and smile. I'll do the talking," instructed Ramsey. "You sure you're okay?"

Majors nodded an okay but the turn signal blinking on the wagon seemed to penetrate his body as though it were his own pounding heartbeat. He braked at the guard's request, keeping the car in gear.

Ramsey stepped out, remaining on the opposite side of the vehicle from the guard. "Afternoon," he smiled to the guard, his .45 tucked neatly in his belt behind his back.

The guard moved silently to the side of the wagon. Majors could smell garlic as he came close to the window to converse across the top.

"Whatcha' need?"

"The name's Price. Kevin Price," lied Ramsey with a southern drawl. "Gotta' do a survey here tomorrow for the new factory. Wonder if ya'll can show us where we can keep our equipment for a few days?"

"Survey? What survey? What company you with?"

"Raven Industries," Ramsey acted surprised. "Didn't they call? Hell, we was 'spoze ta start yesterday but you know how it goes. They shoulda' called ya'll. Damn paper pushers always fuckin' up." He leaned into the window, "Didn't I tell ya Frank. Them fuckers always screwin' up."

Majors nervously nodded agreement, barely hearing what Ramsey said. He was more concerned the guard would see the M-16 pressed between his left leg and the door panel. He felt vulnerable and the heat and garlic aroma from the guard was about to make him nauseous.

The guard glanced into the wagon and Majors' heart shot into his throat.

"Got a truck load of equipment comin' in a minute," Ramsey said loudly to distract the guard's attention. "You just show us a shack where we can lock the stuff up for the night and we'll get all the other shit and the paper work straight in the mornin'. Me and the boys are kinda' petered out, ya know. Been drivin' all day. Like to find us a cold beer and a hot meal. Maybe a few sympathetic hot women. Know what I mean."

"Hang on. I'll see what we got," the guard smiled, returning to his air-conditioned hut.

Ramsey rested his left arm on the top of the wagon. The sun heated metal burned torturously but he suffered the pain, remaining casual as he gripped the .45 pretending to massage his lower back.

The guard was now dialing his telephone and Ramsey knew he had to act fast. Could he kill the man? Was this guy simply a local employee, an innocent citizen? He decided the stakes were too high and he would, as they said in Vietnam, shoot now and let God sort it out later. He slowly pulled the .45 from his belt and cocked it then suddenly the guard's face slammed forward through the shattering glass window that separated them. Behind him stood Eisen, twisting his knife. Eisen lifted an Uzi assault weapon from the dead man's hand, held it up and pointed at it with the bloody knife to demonstrate to Ramsey why he had to eliminate him. He then gave the okay sign.

Ramsey quickly moved to the gate and swung it open. Majors, sweating nervously, leaned his forehead on the steering wheel in relief.

Eisen stashed the guard's body under a desk then quickly got on the radio to his team.

"Are you alright?" asked Ramsey of Majors as he began readying the weapons.

"They've got my boys, Ram. Don't worry about me. I'll do whatever it takes."

"Frank, you've got to prepare yourself for the worst. In case they aren't here, or..."

"We have five minutes!" interrupted Eisen as he jumped in the back seat. "Then the teams hit the hanger. You guys ready?"

"Let's go," ordered Ramsey.

Majors hit the accelerator. The forty-year-old neglected road was cracked and pitted, filled with weeds and growth over which Majors' wagon bumped uneasily but quickly toward the lone aircraft hangar. The wagon came to a slow halt in the shadows of the old barracks nearest the airstrip leaving them with a two hundred yard sprint between the building and the hangar, a distance that looked like miles and a sprint that seemed like an eternity to the three men who had to make it. The only sounds were their footsteps and heavy breathing as the sun beat down torturously and glared in their eyes from the west across the old seasoned runway. It blinded them to any opposition and their lives were at that moment dependent on pure chance and surprise.

Finally they reached the long shadow of the rusty old hangar where Ramsey cautiously approached a window or what once was a window, now only a frame. He rose and peered in carefully, cursing because his eyes had still not adjusted from the bright sun.

Inside the hangar the underside of the corrugated roof loomed high above the greasy cement floor where Carol and the boys huddled at the gunpoint of Whitemoon's man. He said nothing, felt nothing. Behind him three other men hurriedly positioned the three sixteen foot Hawk missiles, securing the mobile launcher just behind the huge hangar doors. Another man programmed an auxiliary control unit that was connected to a satellite receiver dish on the roof.

"Hurry up!" shouted Hard Eyes impatiently.

"I've got to test it," returned the programmer.

"How long?"

"Two… three minutes."

"Make it one," he demanded as he looked at his watch, then turned and started shouting orders throughout the hangar. "Open the doors. Get that damn jet out on the runway. I want to get the hell out of here before the big flash."

Carol sat staring up the barrel of the gun of their guard. The boys stared in amazement at the quick movement of the missile launcher as it was tested then positioned at a skyward attitude.

The missile set up was now complete, all was secure and the long dark-gray shining Hawks, now sporting the raven crest against a pale moon, stood poised for launch.

Young Chris was startled when the huge hangar doors began to roll open and the jet's engines burst alive at the same moment. The sun shot through the doors, its glare blinding, catching everyone unprepared. Hard Eyes turned away from the glare and looked back to Carol. Behind him the jet screamed as it moved slowly from the shadows of the hangar onto the bright hot tarmac.

"What are you going to do with us?" Carol yelled above the noise.

Hard Eyes ignored her.

"You can't hurt these children," she yelled.

He came closer and smiled, "Consider it a mercy killing, lady. It ain't nothing compared to what's gonna' happen in a couple minutes."

Sixteen hundred miles away Whitemoon was pacing the length of the launch control center aboard his sleek white Hatteras. He had flown down immediately after inspecting the unfinished launch site at Green Cove that morning and now worked the room like a caged hungry tiger, back and forth, impatient, deadly. The boat had been gutted and its interior redesigned for this very day. Stripped of her original luxuries and refitted with computer launchers, satellite transmitters, receivers, video monitors, everything he needed to initiate his destructive vengeance. Though Whitemoon appeared calm his mind and dark soul were electrified with anticipation.

"Confirmation from Green Cove is overdue, sir."

Whitemoon turned abruptly, "Are all other systems ready?"

"Yes sir."

"Begin launch count down," he ordered. "Do not discontinue for any reason. Do you understand?"

"Yes sir. Do not discontinue," repeated Whitemoon's technician as he entered the coded signals into a computer.

Above the control board where all aboard the boat could see, a digital readout flashed *3 MIN* then converted to seconds. The crew and Whitemoon remained silent as the seconds ticked off - 180, 179, 178...

On Maryland's eastern shore of the Chesapeake Bay a small vacation cottage on Kent Island came alive with the chiming beep of an auxiliary launch control unit. What appeared to be solar panels on the roof slid aside and a trio of converted nuclear Hawk missiles nosed skyward, their target, Washington, D.C. Near Andalusia, Alabama, an old tobacco barn opened its tin roof. These Hawks were programmed for the Pensacola Naval Air Station. Simultaneously Hawks readied themselves in Cedar Grove, Virginia, target Norfolk. Similar covert launch sites activated near military bases on both coast. Whitemoon could visualize the Hawks in his mind, each strategically placed and targeted, each carrying his raven. He reveled in the simplicity of it all. The Hawks, uncomplicated as missiles go but effective with the Whitemoon package in the nose. And their launch sites childishly deceiving. Like his ancestors, he smiled, deception, surprise and simple aggression to defeat the complex white man's world.

At Green Cove Springs the auxiliary launcher buzzed and beeped as it came alive via a satellite signal.

"It's on! It's activated! The damn firing program is activated!" yelled the programmer.

Hard Eyes turned as the missiles automatically adjusted to precise launch attitude, their targets, Jacksonville Naval Air Station, the Navy Base at Mayport and Cecil Field. Three targets, three missiles and the reason why this was the last site to be completed. It was difficult to program. The alternative would have been three separate launchers, more warheads and more time. Whitemoon could wait no longer.

Whitemoon's men scurried for the jet trying to clear the area before the missiles launched. As they did, Eisen was working his way along the side of the hangar, peeking through windows and making count of the opposition. He figured about thirteen in all, not counting the jet crew. They were all armed with side arms and most sported assault rifles such as the one he discovered at the guard hut, some possessed Russian made AK-47's.

At the rear of the hanger Ramsey and Majors slid through the window and crouched in the shadows. Through the large hanger doors Ramsey could see suddenly coming out of the sun like flying charging bulls, the Navy helicopters clearing the tall pines and cruising in low over the runway. A Navy door gunner strafed the jet, then the front of the hanger with his 60 mm as the second chopper discharged its SEAL team members on the tarmac, firing as they took to the ground.

Hard Eyes turned to the confusion outside. When he turned back he spotted Frank Majors and fired. Majors fell, bleeding from his side.

Ramsey fired a burst in return from his M-16 then had to hold his fire when the man dashed behind the auxiliary launcher control console, snatching and taking young Chris with him as a shield.

Ramsey cursed as he dove to the cover of a workbench by the wall.

Hard Eyes tucked the boy under his arms and began backing out of the hangar.

Ramsey stood, held him in his sights and moved forward determined not to let the boy come to harm and equally determined to end the life of this evil eyed monster.

Another burst from the chopper's door gunner sent rounds near the missile launcher, a man screamed and fell behind Hard Eyes who flinched and turned, giving Carol the opportunity to lunge for his gun and knock the boy free. Chris scrambled to his brother and both sought safety behind the console.

Eisen and one of his team appeared from behind the Hawks, weapons extended. Hard Eyes panicked, shot Carol then turned to be ripped apart by three M-16's. Ramsey stood sweating, wide-eyed, motionless. He had emptied his weapon into the man but late, too late. Carol lay bleeding on the ground, unconscious, probably dead, thought Ramsey.

Outside of the hanger the firefight continued with most of Whitemoon's men already taken down by the Navy team. The jet was now taxiing for escape but found itself blocked by the two hovering helicopters. One chopper slowly moved to the jet's side, its gunner training the 60mm on the cockpit signaling to the jet pilot to stand down but the pilot stubbornly continued. The gunner opened fire, killing the pilot and forcing the aircraft to swerve radically along the runway.

Another of Whitemoon's men attempted escape in the pickup truck. Automatic fire ripped both truck and driver. It swerved and rolled, crashing into the missiles, collapsing the launcher base. The three missiles were now aimed at ground level but still functioning, the countdown still in progress.

Ramsey rushed to Majors. Eisen and his team had already snatched Carol, the boys and their own wounded and fled for safety away from the hangar. They had all barely cleared the large metal structure when the countdown ended and the missiles began to fire. The first soared wildly into the sky at a low angle, slamming into the trees at the edge of the old runway. Its solid fuel exploded like napalm, its warhead destroyed, not having time to arm itself in flight. The second Hawk shot straight onto the runway, bouncing, rolling wildly then smashing into the landing gear of the jet that exploded as it fell crippled to the ground. The missile continued to roll, its fins ripping from the fuselage, sparks and smoke trailing. It snapped at the center, both sections now airborne, exploded with fury as they struck one of the hovering helicopters. The awesome explosion was hellish, creating a wild fireball that consumed men and hot metal then threw them in all directions across the hard tarmac. The explosion also forced the other chopper down, its landing skids spreading and digging into the tarmac, the main rotary blades shattering like balsa as they ripped into the concrete. The chopper twisted then stilled on its side, allowing the surviving crew to climb free.

The remaining Hawk missile was jammed into the side of the overturned pickup truck, launching, then spinning and careening both it and the truck into and across the hanger where it collided with a large pile of drums containing Whitemoon's jet fuel. The missile, truck and fuel exploded with a force that rocked everything for miles, tearing the hanger apart at every seam, nut and bolt, and sending a fireball of flame and steel hundreds of feet in the air.

Ramsey and the others, having taken shelter behind the old barracks, bared the heat and what seemed like hurricane force winds as the explosion seared the old structure and filled the sky.

Eisen was treating Carol's wounds. Another team member treated Majors' while his boys held his hands and stared in silent fear and confusion.

Ramsey stepped out and looked at the still blazing inferno, the heat slamming his face like some relentless heavyweight boxer, the torturous pounding somehow knocking things clearer in his mind. He looked down at Carol, showing no emotion, no concern, not even pity, as Cannon's final words kept running through his mind, 'Don't trust anyone', the dying man said. He turned back to the raging fire and rising black smoke. Anger and a desire for revenge filled his entire being. He tightened his grip on the M-16 hanging at his side. A man's face flashed through his mind and he vengefully squeezed the trigger but nothing happened. He had expended his ammo, his patience and his tolerance of the system he had long served. And, he thought, he would expend the man he now saw in his mind.

Chapter Twenty Eight

The air above and around the strategic military areas on both coasts came alive with frantic action. Aircraft of all services filled the skies and as visual and radar contact was made with Whitemoon's nuclear arrows a chill ran through those who were monitoring the situation in Washington. Most of the missiles were quickly eliminated soon after launch being the general locations of their firing sights were known. The missiles were fast and their targets near however, and on the west coast two of them got through. One failed to arm itself and therefore failed its mission, another, targeted for San Diego, didn't fail. The Navy installation, the city and the population, though not completely destroyed due to the size of the warhead, suffered over sixty per cent casualties.

Washington had been spared as well as Norfolk and the other east coast areas but in the sky above South Georgia, Lieutenant James Meredith, whose squadron was now protecting the new Trident Submarine Base at King's Bay, listened to hasty dialogue as three Hawks ran south along the coast. The flight turned on its targets and the jet age joust began. The F-14 Tomcats were efficient, screaming down on the First Hawk then the next, ironically eliminating missiles originally designed to track, attack and destroy aircraft such as theirs.

The next Hawk was Meredith's. It was his revenge, his forgiving moment. He would now make right the incident in the air above Jacksonville. His mind and his aircraft came together in an uncanny harmony for those transitory moments as he bore down on the determined Hawk. He was clear of thought, free of mental barriers, simply reacting, moving, feeling the precise power of his aircraft.

The Hawk came swiftly, intent on its mission and Meredith could almost sense it, feel it. His aircraft reached out to it as it told Meredith to fire. Now. Now! NOW! the Tomcat screamed and he quickly obeyed with a squeeze of the trigger. His heart raced but then froze when he suddenly realized his own missiles had failed to fire! He tried again and they failed again. His eyes widened and all the fears returned. Save us Jimmy boy! Help us! Don't let us die, Jimmy boy! Now, far in the distance, he could actually see Whitemoon's Hawk missile. It seemed to smile sadistically. Lieutenant James Meredith locked his eyes, his mind and his soul onto the tormenting missile that drew him like a moth to a flame or some mysterious magnetic force. He suddenly found himself smiling as he and his aircraft joined effortlessly, willingly, to bring the Hawk's eminent victory to an end.

Meredith's F-14 and the missile came together in a massive explosion above the bulky sub-tenders at Kings Bay as they sat helplessly docked. The submarines had all hastily put to sea earlier, ordered out during a loading exercise. Had the Hawk completed its mission, the new Navy base itself would not have been a major loss considering it was under construction and consisted primarily of a few block buildings, temporary mobile facilities and minimal personnel but the loss and inaccessibility to the base's cache of trident missiles was another story altogether.

The true significance of Meredith's sacrifice and protection of Kings Bay was that it secured a total defense of the east coast against Whitemoon's hideous scheme. With the death of Lieutenant James D. Meredith, the immediate threat was over and the Whitemoon crisis also died.

The loss at San Diego, though tragic, served as the proving factor convincing the Russians of the truth of the President's message. The message had been brief and factual, stating only the seriousness of the crisis, that it was an in-house situation and there was no time for further rhetoric. "The Russian Premier," said the President, "must accept this communication as truth and consider his obligation to humanity. Should he do otherwise, all the world will become a united Soviet enemy."

Chapter Twenty Nine

A single fighter jet cut through the clouds above the sea. It was gray and carried no numbers, no markings and claimed no nation. Below, the pilot could see Whitemoon's Hatteras running full out across the ocean surface, destined for his private island refuge.

Whitemoon stood cold in the warm tropical wind, glaring at the white bubbly path left by the speeding craft. He'd never known failure and certainly hadn't considered it to any degree in his plan of destruction. He had lost but couldn't and wouldn't accept his lost. The hate was still growing, building, smoldering. He would begin again, he told himself. He would defeat them and have his revenge.

As the glistening white yacht rounded the reef to enter the secure inlet water of Whitemoon's Heritage Place Island the anonymous aircraft banked, dropped closer to the sea and sighted the island hills. It was the pilot's final visual confirmation as he goosed the throttle and rocketed up for more altitude. He then armed the destructive special delivery package, released it, kicked in his afterburners and quickly sped up and away from its target.

Whitemoon, his people and his threat became victims of his own vengeance, lost in a mushroom cloud at the hands of an ally he had never known. The Committee had begun to clean house.

It was evening in Washington and exceptionally cool for the time of summer. Streetlights were silently replacing sunlight and the bustling day traffic was now being replaced with the late workers and those in search of entertainment or dining out.

In a small quaint restaurant of quality in Georgetown a distinguished elderly gentleman drew on his favorite red wine midway through a very pleasing and peaceful dinner. As he dined he thought of many things, broad, substantial matters that spanned his life and his world. He reflected on years past and considered the future, telling himself his was a worthwhile existence that had contributed well to mankind. As he reviewed his life the wine glass was refilled. He sipped it slowly.

In front of the restaurant, a black limousine coasted to a halt at the curb. The fine tuned engine hummed, the reflected lights of passing vehicles sliding along its spotless exterior as it patiently waited.

The gentleman glanced across the restaurant, through the wood sash windows and out to the street. His eyes fixed on the small gold emblem on the black door of the waiting vehicle confirming his expectations. He would consume his dinner first, he thought, his wine and perhaps a small dessert. There was no hurry for he knew they would wait for him. Like the Grim Reaper, he laughed, the limousine would patiently bide its time.

He would complete his dinner and... oh yes, settle up his monthly bill. After these many years of patronage he wouldn't care to leave an unpaid tab. After all, didn't they stock this wine at his request and of course he must leave a note for his dear friend, Laura, the restaurant's owner. She was so kind to him in the late 1930's when he first arrived in Washington. He had no time for her then but he patronized her establishment for nearly fifty years. Should they have married? Did they really love each other, he wondered.

He would dine and pay his bill and write a short note on a napkin then depart this place for the last time. The man who would plot the destiny of the world while watching children in a museum would seat himself comfortably next to a stranger in the grand limousine without concern. Whatever manner they chose to kill him would be painless. He had earned that much respect. He found comfort in the knowledge the Committee would continue, its goal never changing. In addition he somehow oddly found pride in his own death. A cancerous failure must be removed and Whitemoon's failure was his own, he surmised. As such, his failure though unfortunate, required an equal remedy.

Was he a man content with death or tired with life? It was a struggling yet challenging thought as he drank the rich red wine he so cherished for many years, the sweet wine with the subtle painless poison that was now killing him.

Chapter Thirty

Ramsey busied himself with the trays atop the pushcart in the lobby of the third floor of the hospital. He was dressed as an orderly, standing with his back to the elevator.

At the nursing station the female agent disguised as a nurse watched the elevator casually as she too pretended to be doing her usual chores. She was his mirror and would reflect the arrival of their expected visitor. The rest was up to Ramsey. He would have it no other way. "This big fish was his," he said. "This catch was personal. Very personal."

Every time the elevator stopped at the third floor a mild bell would signal its arrival, the door would slide open and its passenger would exit. Hours had passed, the bell ringing over and over again. To Ramsey each ring grew in volume, each becoming more intense, more intimidating and he wasn't sure how much longer he could tolerate this waiting game.

Already on one occasion the nurse had mistaken a staff doctor for their target of reception. She gave the signal causing Ramsey to turn swiftly and come face to face with the man. The doctor stepped aside, ignoring Ramsey's embarrassment. It was soon after Ramsey decided to change his approach. Let the bastard go to her room, he thought. Take it slow and play it to the fullest.

Again the bell rang. Again Ramsey tensed. The nurse smiled as the man approached her requesting the room number of a patient. "Room 316," she answered. "Down the hall to the left."

"Thank you," he replied, then walked around the desk and down the hall.

The nurse picked up the phone. It was the signal to Ramsey who began rolling the cart in the same direction.

As the man neared room 316 he paused to look around and back. Ramsey quickly left the cart and darted through the nearest door. The man continued, then stopped and listened at the door. Determining it was safe to enter, he carefully pushed the door open discovering only a dimly light private room with a single patient. Carol lay motionless, eyes closed, her hair resting on the white pillow reflecting what little light came from the dim lamp above the bed.

The man moved slowly to her side and stood, watching, building his nerve.

Ramsey slid silently into the room from the shared restroom that joined room 318, continuing to the window behind the intruding assassin. His hand tightened on the dangling cord of the window blinds as he watched the man remove a syringe from his coat pocket, pluck off the needle cover then lean over Carol and take hold of the sheet and blanket.

Ramsey waited and watched as the coverings were slowly lifted down to Carol's waist. There was no gown. She was bare and beautiful. The man extended the syringe and plunged it up under her ribs and into her heart. Before he could push the deadly drug through the needle Ramsey broke the silence.

"You're wasting your time, Admiral. She's already dead."

Admiral Peters froze.

"She died this morning," Ramsey stated without emotion.

Peters removed the syringe from Carol's body and turned slowly. "I underestimated you, Commander."

"I appreciate that," said Ramsey. "It kept me alive."

"No," replied Peters. "She kept you alive. She was supposed to terminate you before you got too far."

"Was that before you had the Senator killed, Admiral? Or after?" Ramsey's eyes went cold with resentment. "You lost her, didn't you? After she called you from my house and told you Senator Coggin was there and you sent your people to kill us all. That's when you lost her when she realized how dirty your Committee played ball. When they nearly killed her. She couldn't tell me she was your agent so she helped by giving me computer info. But she was never really yours to start with was she? Like Frederick Dillair. He thought he was working for the Navy but you lost him too when he figured it all out. Like Carol, who was supposed to keep me in check, he was to keep an eye on Whitemoon then you threw in Theresa Coggin and complicated his life. He didn't know about the Committee but he knew enough to see that your people were giving Whitemoon carte blanche, a little too much rope. He figured out your game. His problem was he had no one to turn to."

Peters turned the syringe in his hand as Ramsey continued.

"I was supposed to be your safety valve, right Admiral? I was to go through the motions and conduct an investigation that you could control." Ramsey yanked the cord, using the sunlight to temporarily blind Peters as he drew his .45 and extended it. "How far does the Committee go?" grilled Ramsey.

Peters smiled, "Do you seriously expect an answer?"

"I'm serious enough to kill you, Admiral," said Ramsey, cocking the hammer. "You fucked up. You're a dead man anyway. Your own people will see to that."

"It's too big for you. Too big for anyone."

"Is it?" Ramsey's anger tightened around the .45. "I've seen war. I've smelled it and lived it." He moved along the window. "War is people, Admiral, not Committees. People die like so much beef in a slaughterhouse and if you slaughter the right people you stop the war. Isn't that how it works? The question is, do I begin with you?"

"We're not at war, Commander."

"Oh yes we are, Admiral. Right here. Right now. And you're the enemy and I'm going to blow your fucking brains out just like your people took out Theresa Dillair."

Ramsey stepped toward Peters, the .45 extended. Peters backed against the bed as he began moving away when the door to the room suddenly opened. Startled, he jerked against the bed, the movement causing Carol's arm to fall as though to prevent his escape.

"Ramsey. Son, you can't do this," pleaded Captain Downs from the doorway. "You don't want to have to live with this."

Ramsey glared at the bedside scene. He slowly pressured the trigger with every intention to shoot then Peters smiled as he quickly jammed the syringe into his own heart, injecting the deadly drug. His eyes widened as he gripped his chest.

Ramsey lowered his gun and turned to the window. "I hope it's painful. You bastard, I hope you suffer." He heard the thud as the Admiral fell to the floor.

Epilogue

It was early fall by the calendar but in St. Augustine summer extended itself as usual. The sun was warm and pleasant and the inlet waters were gentle. Ramsey nursed a cold beer as he watched Frank Majors and his oldest son bait live shrimp on their fishhooks. Little Chris, being too impatient to wait out fish, poked around the weedy beach with a faded piece of driftwood.

Ramsey was as content as possible considering recent events. He was no longer in the Navy as far as he was concerned although his discharge was not formal for a few more weeks plus he had gained a little weight and was sporting a respectable tan.

The two young boys had fared well under his care as well while Majors recovered from his wounds. The boys even helped Ramsey pick out a small beach house on a secluded part of the island. In addition he had taken them to Washington and showed them the sights while making arrangements to ship his things and sell his town house. While there, the boys dragged him to the Air and Space Museum three times and were treated to a quick tour of the Pentagon.

At present Ramsey had no plans for the future, no prominent ambitions. He simply desired a little peace but seriously doubted he could ever rest easy with his knowledge of the threat of the Committee.

By now Chris had worked his way back up the inlet shore and was showing Ramsey a small crusted rock, questioning if it could be a piece of Spanish gold like in the movies. Ramsey played along by chipping away the crust to reveal an old bottle cap. For Ramsey it was good for a laugh but to Chris it was a promise of more possible treasure and he quickly darted back for more. Watching the boy scoot down the beach Ramsey spied two men dressed in dull neat suits. Needless to say, they were a little out of place. Now what's wrong with this picture, he thought and tensed as he stood then moved away from the family to intercept them. Majors also saw the men and Ramsey's concern and stood, anticipating trouble.

"Commander Ramsey Lightner?" one of the men questioned.

Ramsey didn't reply but kept moving carefully.

The other man extended an I.D. "Secret Service, Commander. The President would like to see you immediately."

"The President?"

"Yes sir."

"In Washington?"

"No sir. He's waiting at your home."

"My house?"

"Yes sir. With the Russian Ambassador."

Ramsey turned to Majors, "Frank," he yelled. "Gotta' go. Catch a big one and we'll cook him for dinner."

Majors acknowledged and went back to his fishing.

There were three plain sedans parked by the house when Ramsey and his two escorts pulled up. A Secret Service agent stood near one of the cars, another by the front door.

When Ramsey entered he found seated casually around his living room was the President, the Soviet Ambassador,

Captain Downs and the Secretary of State. There was no one else in the house though through the glass patio doors on the beach side he could see two other agents on the sun deck and yet another on the beach.

"Commander," the President stood. "Commander, I'm honored to meet you. Please excuse our presumptuous use of your home. Captain Downs here was sure you wouldn't mind and I'm sure you will understand our reasons for secrecy." The President reached for Ramsey's bewildered hand. "I'd like you to meet Soviet Ambassador Lokovitch, Captain Downs you already know and Secretary of State. Alison Garner.

The President spoke as though this were just an everyday friendly visit. Ramsey looked to Downs for support. Downs returned the gesture with a confident smile.

"How is the fishing, Commander," the Russian Ambassador asked pleasantly as he shook Ramsey's hand.

"Not too good just now," Ramsey returned politely. "But we're working on it."

"We haven't got much time, Commander. The rest of the world thinks we're at Camp David. Please be seated. After all, this is your home," said the President.

Ramsey sat, smiled, "Yes, it is isn't it."

"May I call you Ramsey?" asked the President.

"My friends call me Ram."

"Good. Then I'll call you Ram. I certainly don't want to be your enemy. I hear that isn't very wise," he laughed.

Ramsey smiled in return. He was at a disadvantage and uncomfortable.

"Young man you have done this country a great service," the President continued. "And of course, we are extremely grateful." He paused, growing serious. "But unfortunately we are in need your help again."

"You have uncovered a terrible threat," entered the Soviet Ambassador. "This so-called *Committee* is an enemy that has no country but threatens all people."

"I've reported all I know," said Ramsey. "There's little else I can do."

"Ram," the President leaned forward, "We're faced with a unique problem which calls for an equally unique solution." He paused, sitting back. "And we think you're that solution."

"I don't understand," stated Ramsey. "These people are international. There's nothing..."

"I have established a new defense program," the President interrupted. "A new *Armed Service,* if you will, with all the resources and power necessary for any action necessary. Many other nations of the world have done the same and have agreed to work together to find and fight this common enemy. Commander, you are that new service."

Ramsey's mind raced in a radical emotion he couldn't describe and his first instinct was to burst into laughter but knew these men were serious.

"You'll have the complete cooperation of most all nations," stated the Soviet Ambassador. "Including mine."

"Commander Lightner, we have discovered that this Committee is capable of most anything," came Secretary Garner. "They're influential in the military and governments and industry all around the globe. A large-scale solution to this problem is impossible. We believe you have the motive and ability to serve in this capacity. And you've already proven you're untainted...um, non-Committee. You will also receive all the training and support necessary. Anything and everything, and of course, complete secrecy dictated according to your design and requirements."

Ramsey stood, walked to the patio door and stared out across the ocean. Captain Downs joined him.

"Ram, we have no choice."

"We?"

"I've agreed to head up your base of support."

"But you were going to retire."

"Yeah, and so were you," smiled Downs.

Ramsey turned to the President, "Sir, I need time."

"Of course," the President conceded as he rose, the others following his lead. "Take what time you need, Ram. Give your decision to Captain Downs and then we'll take it from there."

Ramsey shook each of their hands as they departed.

"I hope you catch a big fish," smiled the Russian Ambassador as he departed. "A very big fish."

Ramsey stood on his sun deck above the beach. It had been only a short time since his honored guest departed and it had taken that brief time for him to reach a decision.

Below his home on the beach evening shadowed the dunes, each seeming to come alive as the tall sea oats waved in an off shore wind. The cool salt breeze was cleansing, filling Ramsey's lungs as he inhaled and stretched his arms to rest along the rail.

A lone sea gull screamed, launched itself from the sand and soared into the sky, riding the wind. Ramsey stood alone watching with a smile as he remembered something Carol had told him when they discussed starting over.

"Yeah," she said with childish excitement in her eyes. "Sometimes you just have to ride the wind and see where it takes you."

Ramsey Lightner returns in
The Ram Factor

Also by Frank Mosco

~~~~~~~~~~~~~~~~~~~~~~~~

Fiction

Monkey
Cane's Gate
SHORT, The Last Ghostrider

Nonfiction

Adventures in Black & White, Vol. 1
People, Places & Things

Adventures in Black & White, Vol. 2
Native American Dancers

Screenplays

The Last Jazz
Cane's Gate
A Monkey Tale

For publishing information contact:
quillquestbooks@msn.com